Renew by phone or online
0845 0020 777
www.bristol-city.gov.uk
Bristol Libraries

KT-220-987

PLEASE

BRISTOL LIBRARIES
WITHDRAWN
SOLD AS SEEN

Bristol Library Service

AN 3060296 3

**Welcome to the world
of Sydney Harbour Hospital**

**(or *SHH*… for short—
because secrets never stay hidden for long!)**

Looking out over cosmopolitan Sydney Harbour, Australia's premier teaching hospital is a hive of round-the-clock activity—with a *very* active hospital grapevine.

With the most renowned (and gorgeous!) doctors in Sydney working side by side, professional and sensual tensions run sky-high—there's *always* plenty of romantic rumours to gossip about…

Who's been kissing who in the on-call room? What's going on between legendary heart surgeon Finn Kennedy and tough-talking A&E doctor Evie Lockheart? And what's wrong with Finn?

Find out in this enthralling new eight-book continuity from Medical™ Romance—indulge yourself with eight helpings of romance, emotion and gripping medical drama!

Sydney Harbour Hospital
***From saving lives to sizzling seduction,
these doctors are the very best!***

Dear Reader

I love being part of a continuity series. Not only do I get to work with some fabulous authors, but often there's a bit of a challenge involved. This might be from weaving threads of other stories into my own, or it might come from the characters and their backgrounds that I've been given to work with.

This story gave me a new area to explore. In fiction, that is. I don't think there's anybody whose life has not been touched in some way by the darkness that is depression. It could be a brief acquaintance, or long enough to present one of life's more difficult challenges. It could be ourselves, or someone that we're close to.

This is Zoe's story, and it begins after her world has turned upside down because of postnatal depression. She is lucky enough to meet Teo and their story is… Well, you can judge for yourself. It involves hope, of course, and that's the key to getting out of the dark. Hanging on to hope. It's there and it's real, and if you can hold it close to your heart it will grow.

What better way to find a lovely big piece of hope than through the journey of a romance that has the promise of a happy future?

With love

Alison

SYDNEY HARBOUR HOSPITAL: HOSPITAL: ZOE'S BABY

BY
ALISON ROBERTS

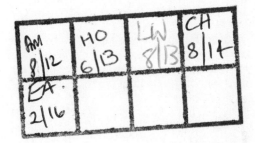

AM 8/12	HO 6/13	LiN 8/13	CH 8/14
EA. 2/16			

For Linda, with much love. And Queenscliff.
The combination that made this story a joy I will never forget.

All the characters in this book have no existence outside the imagination of the author, and have no relation whatsoever to anyone bearing the same name or names. They are not even distantly inspired by any individual known or unknown to the author, and all the incidents are pure invention.

All Rights Reserved including the right of reproduction in whole or in part in any form. This edition is published by arrangement with Harlequin Enterprises II BV/S.à.r.l. The text of this publication or any part thereof may not be reproduced or transmitted in any form or by any means, electronic or mechanical, including photocopying, recording, storage in an information retrieval system, or otherwise, without the written permission of the publisher.

® and TM are trademarks owned and used by the trademark owner and/or its licensee. Trademarks marked with ® are registered with the United Kingdom Patent Office and/or the Office for Harmonisation in the Internal Market and in other countries.

First published in Great Britain 2012
by Mills & Boon, an imprint of Harlequin (UK) Limited.
Large Print edition 2012
Harlequin (UK) Limited, Eton House,
18-24 Paradise Road, Richmond, Surrey TW9 1SR

© Harlequin Books S.A. 2012

Special thanks and acknowledgement are given
to Alison Roberts for her contribution to the
Sydney Harbour Hospital series

ISBN: 978 0 263 22465 8

Harlequin (UK) policy is to use papers that are natural, renewable and recyclable products and made from wood grown in sustainable forests. The logging and manufacturing process conform to the legal environmental regulations of the country of origin.

Printed and bound in Great Britain
by CPI Antony Rowe, Chippenham, Wiltshire

Alison Roberts lives in Christchurch, New Zealand. She began her working career as a primary school teacher, but now juggles available working hours between writing and active duty as an ambulance officer. Throwing in a large dose of parenting, housework, gardening and pet-minding keeps life busy, and teenage daughter Becky is responsible for an increasing number of days spent on equestrian pursuits. Finding time for everything can be a challenge, but the rewards make the effort more than worthwhile.

Recent titles by the same author:

THE NIGHT BEFORE CHRISTMAS
THE TORTURED REBEL*
THE HONOURABLE MAVERICK*
THE UNSUNG HERO*

*Part of *The Heart of a Rebel* trilogy

These books are also available in ebook format from www.millsandboon.co.uk

Sydney Harbour Hospital

Sexy surgeons, dedicated doctors,
scandalous secrets, on-call dramas...

Welcome to the world of Sydney Harbour Hospital
(or *SHH...* for short—
because secrets never stay hidden for long!)

This month enjoy our fantastic medical duo as
new nurse Lily gets caught up in the hot-bed of hospital gossip in
SYDNEY HARBOUR HOSPITAL: LILY'S SCANDAL
by Marion Lennox

Then gorgeous paediatrician Teo
comes to single mum Zoe's rescue in
SYDNEY HARBOUR HOSPITAL: ZOE'S BABY
by Alison Roberts

Don't miss sexy Sicilian playboy Luca
as he finally meets his match this March
SYDNEY HARBOUR HOSPITAL: LUCA'S BAD GIRL
by Amy Andrews

Then in April Hayley opens Tom's eyes to love in
SYDNEY HARBOUR HOSPITAL: TOM'S REDEMPTION
by Fiona Lowe

Join heiress Lexi as she learns to put the past behind her in May...
SYDNEY HARBOUR HOSPITAL: LEXI'S SECRET
by Melanie Milburne

In June adventurer Charlie helps shy Bella fulfil her dreams—
and find love on the way!
SYDNEY HARBOUR HOSPITAL: BELLA'S WISHLIST
by Emily Forbes

Then single mum Emily gives no-strings-attached surgeon Marco
a reason to stay in
SYDNEY HARBOUR HOSPITAL: MARCO'S TEMPTATION
by Fiona McArthur

And finally join us in August as Ava and James
realise their marriage really is worth saving in
SYDNEY HARBOUR HOSPITAL: AVA'S RE-AWAKENING
by Carol Marinelli

And not forgetting Sydney Harbour Hospital's legendary heart
surgeon Finn Kennedy. This brooding maverick keeps his women
on hospital rotation... But can new doc Evie Lockheart unlock the
secrets to his guarded heart? Find out in this enthralling new
eight-book continuity from Medical™ Romance.

A collection impossible to resist!

These books are also available in ebook format
from www.millsandboon.co.uk

CHAPTER ONE

NOTHING had changed.

Zoe Harper released the breath she hadn't realised she'd been holding, in a sigh of pure relief. The sound went unheard thanks to the wail of the siren outside the vehicle she was in.

It could have been yesterday she'd done her last shift as an intensive care paramedic instead of…goodness, how many months ago was it?

Too many.

Enough to have made her afraid that it would feel different. Be impossible, even, given the changes in her life since then. That what had seemed a brave decision could turn out to be disastrous and that it might even send her life tumbling back into a place so awful it was too terrifying to contemplate.

But this was good.

Better than good.

'Traffic's a nightmare.' Her crew partner for the day, Tom, leaned on the air horn and tried to manoeuvre the ambulance through a narrow gap. 'Bet you wish you'd stayed home with the baby a bit longer, eh?'

Being at home with five-month-old Emma instead of heading towards a multi-vehicle pile-up on the south entrance to the Grafton Bridge?

'No way.' Zoe grinned at Tom. 'Bring it on.'

She meant every word.

There was more than relief to be found here.

There was hope.

This was an opportunity to step back into the life she'd always chosen for herself. To shut the door, albeit temporarily, on what had become her new life. But it was about more than simply a job. This was the chance to find out if the person she'd always believed herself to be still existed.

* * *

Working at Australia's premier teaching hospital on the shores of Sydney harbour might be a dream come true but the hospital's central location didn't help when it came to traffic hassles after a consult at one of the suburban hospitals.

And while this new car was superb to handle and its leather upholstery supremely comfortable, no sports car on earth was designed for somebody who was six feet four with the build of a well-conditioned rugby player.

Teo Tuala flexed his shoulders and neck as the traffic inched forward and then came to another complete halt. He could see the flashing lights of emergency vehicles up near the bridge and now he could hear the chop of rotors from an approaching helicopter getting steadily louder.

If they were calling for air transport, it must be a fairly serious accident. Maybe they could use some assistance. Being in the left lane, Teo was able to nudge his sleek car out of the queue of vehicles and onto the motorway shoulder. He flicked his hazard lights on and got out of the confined space. A police officer, edging his way through the traffic jam on a motorbike, swerved into the space he'd created.

He was shaking his head. 'You can't park there, mate.'

'I'm a doctor,' Teo responded. 'Thought they might be able to use a hand up there.'

The young officer's expression changed. 'Hop on,' he offered. 'I'll get you on scene.'

Teo could see why the traffic was so disrupted as he got closer. Three vehicles were involved. One was upside down and partially crushed. Another was wedged between the upside-down car and the bridge supports. The third car was being towed from where it was blocking another two lanes of the highway.

Firemen were using pneumatic equipment to cut into the vehicles. The helicopter was hovering directly overhead, looking for a place to land. There was a background wail of additional emergency service vehicles approaching the scene from the opposite direction. The noise was overwhelming and yet Teo could still hear the shrieks of a terrified person who seemed to be trapped in one of those cars.

And it sounded like a small person.

A quick visual scan of the scene revealed the most senior ambulance officer amongst the knot of police and fire service personnel. The fluorescent vest with 'Scene Commander' on the back was being worn by a woman.

Teo stepped closer. 'Hey, there…'

The woman ignored his greeting. Her attention was still directed to a young, far more junior ambulance officer.

'Have you got access to the back seat?'

'The firies are working on that. That door's jammed as well.'

'And she's trapped?'

'Yes. Her leg's caught under the dash.'

'Get a C collar on her and keep her still until we can extricate her. Stay in the back seat and keep her head immobilised.'

'Zoe?'

The scene commander's head swivelled even further from where Teo was standing as another male paramedic approached. The movement, under the early morning sunshine, sent flickers of colour like small flames through her hair. She had pale skin, he noted, with a scattering of freckles on her nose and the top of her cheeks.

'What's up, Tom?'

'We need you. Oxygen saturation levels on the driver are dropping and there's a kid in a car seat in there as well that we can't get to. Too tight a squeeze for me. The firies reckon they've got the wreck stable. Thought you might be game to crawl underneath.'

The nod came without the slightest hesitation that Teo could detect. 'What status is the child?'

'Can't tell. The seat's upside down and the roof is badly dented on that side. I can see an arm. I reckon it's a toddler more than a baby.'

'I'm a paediatrician,' Teo cut in. 'Can I be of any assistance?'

She looked at him now. Green eyes were assessing him rapidly but with keen attention. He had the impression that he'd passed some kind of test. Pulling off her vest, she handed it to Tom. 'Take over scene control,' she told him. 'There're two more trucks responding and we should be able to start transporting using the northern lanes. The police are clearing an area for the chopper to get down but we'll keep them on standby until we know what's happening with the rolled car.'

She pulled another vest from a container labelled 'Major Incident' and handed it to Teo. 'Put this on,' she ordered. 'And come with me.'

This vest had 'Doctor' on the back. It was a tight squeeze for his large frame but Teo got it on as he followed Zoe. It took only seconds to get amongst the knot of fire officers working on the vehicle. Teo had to watch his feet as he stepped over the thick black cables that connected the cutting gear to the power generators. A blanket marked a patch of ground where a paramedic kit was opened beside a life pack and an oxygen cylinder. Tubing from the cylinder was attached to a bag mask unit being held over the face of the driver by another ambulance officer. A policewoman was holding a bag of IV fluid aloft, its tubing snaking in through the broken window.

'Any change?' Zoe queried.

'Sats down to 95. BP's still dropping. Ninety-five on 60 now. We should be able to get her out any minute.'

Zoe's nod was curt. 'I'll assess her for intubation as soon as she's clear.' She turned to Teo. 'Stay here,' she commanded. 'I'm going to take a few seconds to see if I can get to the child. If it's alive, we'll get it out and I'll hand over to you. The driver's status 1 and I'll need to focus on her.'

Teo knew that meant the victim was in a life-threatening situation. Was it the child's mother? Was the child badly hurt as well? Teo normally saw his patients in the well-controlled environment of a paediatric ward or sometimes the emergency department. This was the first time he'd been on scene in a situation like this. The tension was palpable. The working conditions were astonishing—so many people, so much noise, the smell of fuel and hot metal. How hard would it be to focus?

He watched the redheaded paramedic having a short but intense conversation with a fire officer. She jammed a hard hat onto her head and then lay down, edging herself beneath the wreck of the car's chassis.

Teo felt his breath leave his body in a silent whistle. Not only was it a challenge to focus in this kind of environment but these people were clearly willing to put themselves at considerable physical risk as well. This would be impressive at any time but the actions of this woman called Zoe were positively mind-blowing.

Because she was female?

Teo was ashamed to have to admit that was partly true but there was more to it in this case. Maybe it had something to do with this particular woman. With her striking colouring and those unusually obvious freckles on her skin that made her seem…younger? More vulnerable?

It wasn't a word he should even think of associating with a person who was clearly in command of such an intense situation but, oddly, it stuck somewhere in the back of his head as he stood there, his gaze fixed on the steel-capped black boots he could see protruding from this side of the vehicle. They were moving. Turning as Zoe was positioning herself inside what had to be an impossibly small space to work in. He could hear the muffled, shouted conversation she was having with firemen on the other side of the wreck.

They repositioned their equipment. The 'jaws of life' were used to cut through a central pillar on that side of the car and metal was being peeled back like the top of a spaghetti can. Teo's view was obstructed by the wheels of the wreck and then by the surge of rescuers that moved in.

There was more shouting, the wreck rocked a little and then, less than a minute after Zoe had disappeared beneath the wreck, he saw the car seat being lifted clear and passed from one set of arms to another. It was carried towards him and suddenly Teo realised that it was actually easy to focus in the messy, dangerous environment. All you needed was a patient who needed you. This car seat had a small body strapped inside it. A baby about twelve months old. A boy who was not only alive but fully conscious. His eyes were wide open and frightened as he looked right back at Teo.

'Put him down here,' Teo said. He crouched beside the car seat and reached for the central buckle. 'Hey, there, little one...'

The driver of the car was freed from the wreckage moments after the baby seat had been extricated.

What a stroke of luck, having a paediatrician on scene. Not that Zoe would have had trouble coping but it was an undeniable relief not to have to deal with a baby just yet. That might well blur the comforting demarcation she was establishing between her private and professional life.

She would far rather attend to the female driver and deal with the life-threatening injuries that were immediately apparent as they transferred her from the back board onto a stretcher. She had a collarbone and ribs that had shattered and caused major lung damage on one side. Zoe had to intubate the woman to secure her airway and then do a needle decompression to relieve the increasing pressure from air and blood accumulating in her chest, which could stop her breathing altogether.

Even then, Zoe wasn't happy with how well the woman was breathing. Her blood pressure was still dropping as well and that might indicate further internal injuries.

'I'd like to go with her in the chopper,' she informed Tom when he joined the team assisting her in stabilising this patient for transport. 'I'd prefer to monitor that tension pneumothorax myself if the air rescue team don't mind.'

'We don't mind,' one of the helicopter paramedics said over his shoulder. 'You can party with us any time, Red.'

Zoe had never liked the nickname, earned thanks to her bright auburn hair colour, but the way it pulled her back in time was welcome. She still belonged in this world. It was Tom who would be most affected, however. 'Would you be OK to meet me at the hospital?' Zoe checked.

'Shouldn't be a problem. I'll let Control know, borrow a crew member from one of the other trucks and we'll transport the baby.'

'Oh…' It was the first moment Zoe had had to think about the child since her relief in finding it, hanging upside down in the car seat, but conscious and alert. 'How's he doing?'

'Teo's happy.'

'Teo?' The name was unusual.

'The paediatrician from the Harbour. Nice guy.'

'Mmm.' Zoe shifted her gaze. So his name was Teo? She had noticed the dark olive skin, of course, and the broad features that suggested he was Polynesian.

Right now, he had the baby, wrapped in a blanket, in his arms. He didn't notice Zoe's glance because he was looking down at the child. And…he was smiling. He was also radiating an aura of calmness. As if it was nothing out of the ordinary to be holding a baby at the scene of a major accident. As if he was actually *enjoying* it.

She was close enough to be able to hear if the baby was crying and she couldn't hear even a whimper. Zoe wouldn't have been the least bit surprised if she'd walked over there to find that the baby was smiling back up at him and, for some inexplicable reason that was irritating.

'What's the baby's status?' It came out almost as a snap.

OK, maybe the reason wasn't that inexplicable. How was it that this guy—who looked as if he was a rugby star or a bouncer at some night club or something—could make it look as if caring for a baby was easy. *Fun*, even, when she was a mother, for heaven's sake, and that kind of calmness or pleasure was…unimaginable.

It took an effort to tune in to what Tom was saying in response to her terse query.

'All checked out fine. Totally protected by the car seat, probably, but he'll need observing for a while. Teo says he'll drop into ED as soon as he gets his car clear of this traffic jam and make sure he gets a thorough assessment.'

Zoe turned away from the sight of the big man cuddling an uninjured child. She should thank him for his assistance but she had more important things to do for the moment and maybe she'd catch him later in the ED anyway. She checked the monitor display on the life pack as the helicopter crew secured it to the stretcher her patient was now strapped onto.

'Let's get moving,' she said.

'Hold up…' A police officer was hurrying towards them. 'This is her handbag. You might want her details. Her name's Michelle Drew, aged 34.'

'Thanks.' Zoe took the bag. 'Any next-of-kin details?'

'We're trying to contact her husband. We'll direct him to the hospital. You going to the Harbour?'

Zoe nodded, already moving to follow the crew. The stretcher was rolled swiftly to the back of the waiting chopper and then smoothly loaded. The doors were pulled shut and the rotor speed picked up until they lifted clear of the scene for the short run to the central city hospital.

Zoe had to suppress a smile at the adrenaline rush of being airborne as she moved to help monitor this critically ill patient. The smile was still there inside, though, as she took a quick glance down at the scene they were leaving.

She was more than ready for this kind of a party. She had missed this life *so* much.

The mass of vehicles and people grew rapidly smaller as they gained height but one figure stood out from the rest. The big man with the baby still in his arms. He was looking up, she noticed, watching them take off.

'Pressure's still dropping,' The voice came through the earphones in her helmet. 'Zoe, can you see if you can get another line in?'

By the time Teo walked back to where he'd parked his car on the motorway shoulder, the traffic was moving again. It took less than thirty minutes for him to get to a parking space at Sydney Harbour Hospital and walk into the state-of-the-art emergency department via the ambulance bay.

The triage nurse, wearing a headset with earphones and a microphone, looked up from directing the latest ambulance arrival to smile at Teo. There were more smiles as he went into the department. He'd learned a long time ago that the medical staff on the front line appreciated that a head of department took an interest in patients from the moment they arrived and, whenever possible, Teo would answer a call for a consult from the paediatric department instead of sending a junior doctor.

He went towards the glass board that had the ever-changing details of what patient was where. A glance to his left showed that the major trauma resuscitation area was crowded with staff. The bright red overalls of the helicopter rescue medics were on one side of the room as they observed what was happening with the patient that had to be the woman from the crushed car. His patient's mother.

Did that mean that the intensive care paramedic was still here as well? Zoe? He'd seen her leap into the helicopter. Superwoman. Directing a major incident one minute, crawling into a wrecked vehicle the next and then winging her way to the helipad here. Teo hadn't missed what she'd been doing in between either. The intubation and chest decompression on that woman couldn't have been easy procedures but they'd been done well and had undoubtedly saved a life.

Zoe wasn't in the resus area, however. He could see her standing quietly on one side of the huge glass board, scanning it for information. On the other side of the board, at the other end, were two other people, intently in conversation.

Teo knew both of them. Finn Kennedy was a neighbour, of sorts. He had the penthouse in the Kirribilli View Apartments, a nearby complex that many of the staff, including Teo, lived in. Finn was also the director of surgery here at the Harbour and was probably as frequent a visitor to this department as Teo was, but he knew that Finn's visits were far less welcome. No one could deny Finn's brilliance but it came with a price. Only the ignorant or very confident would attempt to stand up to this man and the person talking to him right now was definitely in the latter category.

Evie Lockheart, reputedly a rising star amongst the ED doctors, was also a resident at Kirribilli View, where she shared an apartment with another junior doctor, Mia McKenzie. Teo would have known about her anyway, however, because her family had the status of royalty around this place. Evie was the great-granddaughter of the man who had founded this hospital and, according to the rumour mill, it was now her father's generous contributions that kept the Harbour amongst the most prestigious teaching hospitals in Australia. Teo had heard that there was no love lost between Finn and Evie but what he was seeing right now made him pause.

'Send her to CT first,' Finn was saying. 'I'll have a theatre free in thirty minutes. It'll take that long to see what you're dealing with.'

'It'll take less time than that for her to crash. She's got a haemothorax that's barely under control. We're losing fluid as fast as we can load it. There's an arterial bleed going on in there.

She's lost the pulse in her right arm and she could lose the limb if we can't get in and deal with the damaged artery. *Now*, Mr Kennedy, not in thirty minutes.'

'And what is it, exactly, that you want from me, Dr Lockheart?'

What indeed? It wasn't the conversation that was piquing Teo's interest. It was more the way they were standing.

Too close?

Or maybe it was the way they were looking at each other. If he didn't know better, he'd think that that kind of eye contact was about something a lot less professional than juggling a theatre queue. It was ridiculous but it was making him feel like he was eavesdropping on a private conversation. Maybe he should step away. But Zoe was here. Was she listening too? A sideways glance seemed to coincide with exactly the same movement from the paramedic. For a split second they held the eye contact and he knew they were on the same wavelength. Teo stepped closer.

'I've just come in to check on the baby,' he said quietly. 'Do you know where he is?'

They both turned back to scanning the board. The department was clearly very busy. Dozens of boxes were filled with the scrawl of marker pen.

The voices on the other side of the board were fainter now.

'But didn't one of your recent edicts stipulate that there would always be a theatre kept free for emergencies from this department?'

Evie Lockheart wasn't a short woman. In the heels she was wearing now, she was only a few inches shorter than Finn's six feet or so. And the way she was holding herself at this moment made her seem even taller.

'There is. You're using it. Plus one of mine for that ruptured spleen you sent up ten minutes ago.'

'You've got a patient in Theatre 5 who's about

to go in for an elective procedure that could easily wait. They haven't started the anaesthetic and they're standing by for a green light from you to set up for Michelle Drew.' To her credit, Evie wasn't sounding smug. In fact, she seemed to have just the right note of reason and deference in her voice. She also sounded extremely persuasive.

Finn wasn't about to be a soft touch for anyone, especially a pretty young woman. His body language was defensive, to say the least. Was Evie about to have her head bitten off in public for interfering with his job? It hadn't been that long ago, in the wake of a discussion about funding cuts, that Teo had heard Finn make some disparaging comment about applying for a few more of the Lockheart millions seeing as their princess was currently a member of staff. But while Finn was giving Evie a glare that could have shrivelled steel, he was far too professional to lose his temper in here.

'Fine,' he snapped. 'I'll sort it.'

Evie's smile lit up her face. 'Fantastic. Thank you so much, Dr Kennedy.' She whirled away from him, heading back to the trauma resus area.

Finn stared at her back for a moment longer before swinging away himself, to head for the nearest telephone.

'Um…' Zoe cleared her throat beside Teo. 'I think your patient's in cubicle 4. Look…eleven-month-old boy from MVA. His name is Harry.'

'Cool. I'll go and see what they've found.' He lowered his voice. 'I might need to pull a few strings and get the little guy admitted.'

'Why would you do that?'

Teo didn't have a chance to answer as a nurse came up to the board with an eraser and a pen. She filled in an empty slot to show that a patient had just come back from CT.

'That was the woman from your scene,' she told Zoe. 'Good job you immobilised her. She's got cracked vertebrae C4 and 5. Could have ended up quadriplegic if they'd been displaced.'

Then she smiled. 'Hi, Teo. We heard you were involved in a bit of action. Your baby's in cubicle 4 if you want to go and see him.'

'Thanks.' Teo returned the smile. 'And it's only a rumour, Louise. I'm not really the father.'

Louise giggled. Zoe didn't even smile. In fact, she was staring at him as if that tiny bit of flirting was just as unprofessional as the spat they'd overheard between Finn and Evie.

Suddenly, it seemed important to do some damage control. 'You're Zoe, aren't you?'

'Yes. Zoe Harper.'

'We didn't get the chance for a proper introduction, did we?' He held out his hand and gave her his best smile. 'I'm Teo Tuala.'

Her expression softened. 'And I didn't get the chance to thank you for your assistance.' Her hand was surprisingly soft. And small. It disappeared completely within his huge, brown paw. Teo gave it a gentle, friendly squeeze and let go.

Behind them, a team of people was swiftly manoeuvring the bed that Michelle Drew lay on towards the internal doors and the lift that would take her up to Theatre.

'How's she doing?' Teo asked.

'Touch and go. She really does need to get into surgery.' Zoe was watching his face. 'Why did you say that you'd find a way of admitting the baby even if he didn't need it?'

Teo rubbed the side of his nose. 'That's not what I said.'

'It sounded like it was what you meant.'

He smiled at her again. 'OK, I confess. I want to make sure he's got family to go to while his mum's in here. It's no secret that I'm not a fan of foster-care.'

Zoe's gaze flicked away. She was looking over his shoulder. 'Tom. You ready to hit the road?'

'Absolutely. Hi, Teo. You'll be happy to know that little Harry's been cleared. His dad's on the way here now. And his grandma, apparently.'

'Couldn't be happier,' Teo nodded. 'I'll go and see him now before I get any later for my rounds. Good to meet you both.'

Zoe watched him walk away, heading for cubicle 4.

She was trying very hard to suppress a niggly sensation in her gut that had the potential to undermine how good her first day back at work had been promising to be.

She recognised the niggle all too well.

Guilt, that's what it was.

Good grief… Teo Tuala was prepared to cross professional boundaries if necessary to prevent a child going into temporary foster-care.

What would he think if he knew that *she* had considered foster-care as an option for her own child?

That she'd gone even further than that and considered giving up her child for adoption?

He'd think she wasn't fit to be a mother.

And maybe she'd have to agree with him.

CHAPTER TWO

'OH…*no*!'

The baby's face puckered in dismay at the tone of Zoe's voice. Hastily, she picked her up and held her, patting the tiny back. 'It's OK, Emma. Don't cry. *Please* don't cry.' She alternated the pats with some soothing circles. 'Come on, we'll find a clean suit for you and we can still be on time for our appointments.'

It took no time at all to find what she needed in Emma's room. Stretchy suits and singlets were folded and sorted according to size and colour in the dresser drawers. The change table was clean to the point of sterility with the wipes, creams and disposable nappies neatly encased in the plastic partitions of the slide-out drawer.

'No more spit-ups,' Zoe commanded, snapping the fasteners on the clean, pink suit.

Emma waved chubby fists and grinned up at her mother. Zoe sighed but stretched out to smooth back wisps of golden hair from the baby's forehead. 'At least you look like someone really loves you.'

Zoe loved her. She *did*. The only problem was that the realisation was in her head and not in her heart. She knew she loved her daughter. She just couldn't *feel* it.

There was no time to change her own shirt. Zoe dabbed at the milky stain with a wet cloth and then abandoned the attempt. Emma had an appointment at the paediatric clinic for a routine check-up. Zoe had an appointment with her psychologist, John Allen, which was hopefully also routine but being late for either appointment was not an option. She had to convince everybody that things were going brilliantly on the home front otherwise John might change his mind about it being a good idea for her to be back at work part time.

And it might have been only a few days since she'd started work again but Zoe already knew that it was the way forward for both herself and Emma. She wouldn't survive being a full-time mother on her own. Not now, when she'd been reminded of the person she'd once been. Not while the memories were still so fresh of how hard it had been in the mothering unit when she'd had support available 24/7.

With the confidence that stepping back into her old life for limited periods was providing, she was getting stronger. She could leave her failures behind her when she was on the road and, when she was at home, she could go through the motions of being a perfect mother and only she knew that she was counting the hours until she could be away from her child again.

Besides, she wanted to be a mother that someone could be proud of. There was nothing wrong with that, was there?

Emma's car seat had a handle with several brightly coloured toys attached by elastic cords. When the soft toys were tugged they made noises. The yellow duck quacked and the lime-green frog croaked. The cow bell was proving popular this morning and it jingled at regular intervals as Zoe drove towards Sydney Harbour Hospital. The noise could have become irritating but Zoe had other things to worry about.

Pulling up at a set of traffic lights, she checked the nappy bag on the passenger seat beside her. Had she remembered the bottle of formula? After spitting up half her breakfast, Emma could well be hungry again by the time they got to the paediatric clinic's waiting room. The last thing Zoe needed was having to try and cope with a fractious baby under the watchful gaze of all the other mothers who would be there.

Mothers who would probably all be like that dreadful support group John had talked her into going to on one occasion. Women who adored their babies and knew what they were doing. Women who never ever felt an inkling of the panic and despair that Zoe had lived with every day since Emma's birth five months ago.

Before that, even. Well before that. Right back in the earliest stages of this whole nightmare when she had agonised over whether even to continue with the pregnancy or not. And when it had all become too much and James had simply walked away. Not that she could blame him. They'd been doing no more than dating casually when she'd become pregnant and while they'd tried to make a go of a relationship, there had been no way James was cut out to deal with the emotional wreck Zoe had morphed into.

Just like her mother.

Oh…rubbish. Zoe parked the car and made a determined effort to park that train of thought at the same time. If she didn't she might blurt something out in her session with John and that would be worse than having Emma screaming inconsolably in the waiting room. She wasn't going to discuss her mother with anyone. She wasn't even going to allow herself to think about her.

The waiting area was packed to the gills this morning. The place was cluttered with prams and strollers, toddlers fighting over the rather sad collection of toys available and babies crying. One distressed infant was pacified quickly by the offer of a breastfeed and Teo smiled at the mother.

Another baby was crying more loudly. Teo took a glance over his shoulder before he disappeared into the examination room.

And then he paused with his hand halfway to pushing the door open and took another look.

It couldn't be.

But it was.

Zoe Harper was in the waiting area and it was her baby who was distressed. Zoe was pacing back and forth, with the infant upright in her arms, tucked against her shoulder. Her head was bent, almost as if she was shielding the baby from view but Teo could see the way Zoe was scanning the area in an oddly furtive manner. She seemed embarrassed that her baby was crying but why? That's what babies did. It was part of their job description.

Maybe Zoe wasn't, in fact, the mother.

Teo dismissed the thought as he entered the examination room. Either the woman he'd seen in total command of a major incident the other day had an identical twin or Zoe had been left in charge of someone else's baby. Her sister, or a friend perhaps, who'd ducked off to go to the loo. That would explain the total lack of confidence he had sensed.

It took only a minute or two to confirm that his registrar had, indeed, picked up an abnormal murmur in a toddler's heart sounds. It took several more to reassure the parents that it wasn't necessarily anything to panic about but then Teo was able to leave the room, confident that his registrar could arrange the urgent tests needed so they would know exactly what they were dealing with. He knew he'd been a little abrupt compared to the time he would normally have spent on a consult like this but he would see the parents again as soon as the results came in.

And he had the strongest desire to check the waiting room again on his way back up to the ward.

This was Zoe's worst nightmare.

The clinic appointments were running late, the area was getting more and more crowded and she just couldn't stop Emma crying. It felt like it had been going on for hours now and the looks she was getting from other mothers had gone from sympathetic to pitying to frankly annoyed. Emma's shrieks had changed as well and the wails were now interspersed with that hiccupping sort of sound that advertised pure misery.

She'd changed her nappy, cuddled her, walked

her up and down and now she was trying to feed her with the bottle of formula she'd mixed before leaving. Emma was having none of it. Her tiny hands were shoving at the bottle containing milk that had a totally unacceptable lack of warmth and small legs were kicking in outrage. Zoe could feel herself being watched. She could feel her face flushing and her shoulders hunching.

'*Please*, Emma,' she whispered. 'Please have a drink.'

Her baby's face took on a deeper crimson hue as Emma went rigid in her arms, arching her little back to produce the loudest crying Zoe had ever heard. What was wrong with her? What was *she* doing that was so wrong? Despair was enveloping her now and, to her horror, Zoe felt tears slipping down her own cheeks. She squeezed her eyes shut as she sensed someone approaching. A staff member, probably, coming to take her child away and give it to someone who could be a better mother.

The touch of a hand on her shoulder was so unexpected that Zoe's eyes snapped open. And then she blinked. Crouched in front of her, so that he was on the same eye level, was Teo Tuala. He wasn't looking at her as if she was some kind of a monster mother either. He was smiling.

'Someone's not happy,' he said. 'Maybe I can help?'

Zoe had noticed what a big man Teo was but having him hunched in front of her like this made him seem like a huge, solid rock of a man. And he had the most extraordinarily dark brown eyes. Eyes that reflected his smile but with a depth that told her he understood that it wasn't just the baby that was so unhappy.

And he wanted to help. Zoe's brain provided a snapshot of the day she'd met Teo. When he had been standing in the middle of a chaotic accident scene holding a stranger's baby and looking as if it was nothing out of the ordinary. As if there was nothing about babies he couldn't cope with. Enjoy, even.

Something else came with that flash of memory. An instinctive sureness that she could trust him. And he was a paediatrician. Something had to be wrong with Emma for her to be crying like this. Without giving herself any time to think of the possible consequences, Zoe pushed her baby towards him. She didn't say a word. She couldn't. If she opened her mouth she would probably start sobbing as hard as her tiny daughter was.

Teo didn't even blink. He took Emma and made her look as tiny as a newborn in his big arms. He got to his feet and peered down at the baby as he rocked her.

'What's the story, little one?' he asked casually. 'It's not so bad around here, really.'

Emma hiccupped, staring up at this new person. And then, miraculously, she stopped howling.

Zoe could hear the sigh of relief coming from more than one of the other mothers around her.

And she had never felt more of a failure. She'd been doing her very best here for so long and it had taken less than thirty seconds for someone else to soothe her baby. A man.

She couldn't look at Teo. She stared down at the bottle of unwanted milk in her hands, her vision blurred by tears.

'Hey...'

Teo was still smiling, she could hear it in his voice. It was a gentle, soothing word that meant nothing but managed to contain an entire message. A 'here we are and it's not really all that bad, is it?' kind of message.

Emma was probably smiling back at him by now.

'Zoe?'

Looking up, Zoe knew instantly that the 'Hey' had been directed at her and not Emma. But she couldn't respond. He might think things weren't so bad because Emma had stopped crying but, for her, things were even worse.

And he knew that. Holding Emma securely with one arm, he reached down and picked up the handle of the car seat. 'Come with us,' he invited softly. 'You can bring the bag.'

Zoe still felt she could explode with the emotion she was trying to contain but she had no choice. She had to follow because 'us' was this paediatrician and *her* baby. And everybody, absolutely everybody in this waiting room, was watching. All the mothers, a sprinkling of fathers, the receptionists and nursing staff behind the desk. Even the older children present were all staring.

But not at her, Zoe realised. They were all watching Teo and the majority of watchers had smiles on their faces.

Because Emma was finally quiet?

Because the sight of such a masculine figure holding a small baby was guaranteed to tug at heartstrings?

Or did it have something to do with the fact that this particular masculine figure was so good looking? It was more than the combination of even features and glossy black hair. There was something about the way Teo handled his size. The grace that came from not only confidence but a relaxed way of looking at life. And it was about the way he smiled so easily and the way he could see solutions rather than problems.

Zoe wasn't the only person following Teo. A little boy had abandoned the toy he'd been playing with and was trotting purposefully in the wake of the big man. His mother had to jump up and catch him before they reached the door.

Teo led her out of the waiting room and along a corridor. Then he opened the door of a room marked 'Private'. There were comfortable chairs in here, a change table, a big basket of toys and a tiny kitchenette. The coffee table had a large box of tissues on it.

'This is a room reserved for families who

need a bit of time out or a special consulta-
tion,' Teo told her. 'It was a bit crowded out
there, wasn't it?'

Zoe's nod was jerky. Her tears had stopped
for the moment but she heard herself sniff. She
pulled a few tissues from the box, blew her
nose and then dabbed at her eyes, hoping Teo
wouldn't notice.

He didn't appear to. He was looking down
at Emma. 'So who's this little sweetheart?' he
asked.

'Her name's Emma.'

'She's, what, about six months old?'

'Nearly.'

'And...she's yours?'

'Yes.' Zoe had noticed the hesitation and it
made her feel ashamed. Was the lack of a normal mother-child bond so obvious?

Emma chose that moment to start grizzling,
too, as if the confirmation that Zoe was her
mother was disturbing. Zoe stared down at the
bottle of milk she was still carrying.

'You could heat that up a bit,' Teo suggested. 'There's a microwave over there beside the coffee-making stuff.'

'We can't stay.'

'Why not?'

'Emma's got an appointment at the clinic. We've been waiting for ages so it must be nearly her turn.'

'That's not a problem. I can make sure she gets seen. Is there something you're worried about?'

'No. It's just a routine check-up.'

'So it's not urgent.'

'Well, no…except…'

'Except what?' Teo prompted.

'I…um…I've got an appointment myself. At 10.30.'

'Obstetric?'

'No.' Zoe didn't want to tell him. She could feel the flush of embarrassment colouring her cheeks. It was one of the worst things about being a redhead, the way blushes came so quickly.

'Sit down, just for a minute,' Teo said. 'Please. You won't be late. This clinic goes on for hours and you can always bring her back after you've been…wherever it is you need to go.'

He could see a solution for everything. And it didn't matter if she didn't want to tell him anything. In the short silence that followed, Teo sat down in one of the chairs. Emma was quiet again. She looked as if she'd fallen asleep in his arms, too exhausted by her misery to remember she was hungry. Zoe sank down onto the edge of another armchair, feeling defeated. There was no point in denying she had a problem. Teo had seen it for himself. He had been prepared to help her in what had been her worst moment for a very long time. He deserved some honesty.

'I have an appointment with John Allen,' she admitted. 'He's a—'

'Clinical psychologist,' Teo nodded. 'I know

John well. He's a good friend. He and his wife Susie live in the apartment next to mine.'

Oh…help. Zoe took in a shaky gulp of air. 'I'd rather he didn't know about what you saw in the waiting room.'

Teo looked curious. 'What did I see?'

'Someone who was being a miserable failure trying to look after her baby,' Zoe muttered.

Teo shook his head. 'I saw a mother doing her best in difficult circumstances. Babies are very good at picking up vibes. What I didn't see was anyone offering you any kind of assistance and I have to say that was disappointing. This is my department and I'm going to have something to say about that at the next staff meeting. You know what?'

'No…' Zoe's response was cautious. She couldn't believe he was being so non-judgmental. Giving her credit, even, for the meltdown he'd rescued them from.

'I think I'll send out a memo. I can do that, 'cos I'm head of department here. Someone might even read it and take some notice.' Teo's smile was fading and his tone became a lot more serious. 'I saw something else, too,' he added.

Oh, no…*he* was the head of the paediatric department? If he did say something to his friend John, her psychologist would certainly take some notice. Zoe gnawed on her bottom lip, hoping she didn't look as anxious as she was now feeling. What else had he noticed?

'I saw someone who lacked confidence in what she was doing,' Teo said gently. 'And while there's nothing unusual in that when it comes to first-time mothers, in your case it astonished me.'

Zoe wished the floor would just open up and swallow her. This was unbearable.

'You want to know why?'

Not really, Zoe wanted to say. She didn't want to hear about just how inept she had looked.

Teo took her silence for assent. 'Because I saw you for the first time only a few days ago and you know what?'

'No...' Zoe almost smiled. She could play this conversational game, especially if he was going to say something nice after getting her to admit her ignorance about what he was going to say.

'I thought you were Superwoman.'

Zoe blinked. *'What?'*

'Superwoman,' Teo repeated. 'There you were, directing that accident scene, hurling yourself into a mangled wreck of a car, show-ing off some not inconsiderable skills in getting that woman's airway and breathing sorted, and then you jumped into a helicopter and took off. All in all, it was a breathtaking performance. You should be proud of yourself.'

It was more than a nice thing to say. Zoe could feel an unfamiliar glow happening inside. She *was* feeling proud of herself. For the first time in *so* long. She ducked her head, embarrassed by the sincere praise. Or maybe it was the frank admiration she could see in those dark eyes that was so disconcerting.

'You made it look easy,' Teo continued. 'Just another day at work.'

'It was. Kind of…'

'Kind of?'

'It was my first day back since…oh, since I was about six months pregnant and I was beginning to think I'd never be allowed to go back.'

'Why not?'

'Because…um…I got postnatal depression after Emma was born.' There. She'd said it. She risked a quick glance at his face. The admiration would be gone, for sure. Probably replaced with that wary look people got at the mere whiff of mental illness.

But Teo's face hadn't changed. 'Badly?'

Zoe stared down at her hands. 'Yeah…I got hospitalised and given some pretty heavy-duty drugs. And then I went into a mothering unit for a while. I'm back home now but…it's still hard.'

'Of course it is. Being a mother is hard enough without the extra challenge of PND.'

Zoe just nodded, glancing at her watch. If she

left now, she could still make her appointment with John in time, but she didn't want to leave Teo with this negative image of her. It would be far better if he continued thinking of her as Superwoman.

'When I'm at work,' she confided shyly, 'I'm me. The me I used to be. The me I recognise. It's when I'm at home that it's different and it's in places like this when I know the other mothers are watching me and judging me that it's the hardest of all.'

She looked up at smiled. 'Thank you for helping,' she said quietly. 'I don't think you know how much it means.'

'It was a pleasure, Zoe. I'm sure you've got a ton of friends supporting you but if you ever need an extra, I'll be here.'

'Thanks.' Zoe wasn't about to tell him that all her friends were in the ambulance service, mostly younger than her, and being in the company of a baby was only marginally less attractive than being in the company of a depressed woman. Let him think she was popular and well supported—in between her stints as Superwoman.

The fantasy was so far from the truth it was amusing enough to bring a genuine smile to her face as she took Emma and tucked her back into her car seat. Emma, bless her, didn't wake up. Then she shoved the things threatening to spill from the pockets of the nappy bag back into place and she was ready to go.

'Can you manage all that?' Teo asked. 'I could wander up with you, if you like.'

'No, thanks.' The last thing Zoe wanted was for John to realise she had a connection to someone he knew on a personal basis. Professional confidentiality was all very well but it didn't apply between doctors, did it? 'I can manage.'

'Of course you can.' Teo smiled again as he held the door open for her. 'What I will do is have a word with the receptionist. They'll slot you in for Emma's appointment as soon as you get back from seeing John.'

* * *

Teo was busy for the rest of the morning and all afternoon that day.

A three-year-old boy, Timmy, who'd been burnt by climbing into a bath of scaldingly hot water was in the paediatric intensive care unit. Teo was part of the team led by Luke Williams that was having to deal with the complications of hypovolaemic shock caused by fluid loss from the burns. It was the child's kidney function that was causing concern today and haemodialysis had to be added to the plethora of procedures that was keeping the small boy alive.

Timmy's mother was beside herself with guilt and fear.

'I had to feed the baby,' she sobbed. 'I had no idea that Timmy was trying to be helpful and run his own bath. I always, always run the cold tap first and then add hot water. I thought he was watching TV in the lounge room. The baby's got colic and she's really hard work after a feed.'

Teo could only listen and imagine how hard

this had to be for her. There was no point in laying blame when it could only make things worse for everyone.

'His dad walked out on us when I got pregnant again. One kid was bad enough, he said. He couldn't handle having two.'

Teo made a sympathetic sound but part of his mind was wandering. Where was Emma's dad? Zoe hadn't mentioned a partner and he'd heard what sounded like a fierce determination to cope with her own situation. On her own. Had she been wearing a ring? He made a mental note to have a look next time he saw her.

Except he had no reason to see her again, had he?

The realisation was curiously disappointing and it stayed with him for the rest of the day as he did his rounds, checking on his small patients and comforting distressed parents. Zoe intrigued him. That she could be so competent in one area of her life and so lost in another made it seem like there had to be a key to unlocking the barrier dividing the areas. And it was sad that it was the home and family side that she was struggling with because Teo knew that was, by far, the most important part of anybody's life. If Zoe could find it, she might not feel the need to be at work at all during this crucial stage of bonding with her baby and then, later, she could have the best of both worlds.

The final task of his day took him back to the paediatric outpatient clinic. Empty of patients now, there was only a cleaner pushing a vacuum cleaner around the chairs and a weary-looking receptionist filing paperwork at the desk.

'Busy day, huh?' He smiled at the receptionist. This wasn't the time to take anybody to task for leaving a distressed mother and child without assistance while they had been waiting.

'It was a nightmare,' the receptionist said. 'One registrar got called away for something on the ward and another had to deal with a kid who had an epileptic seizure in the toilets and we were running *so* late.'

'Did Zoe Harper come back again with Emma?'

'Yes.' The girl gave him a curious glance. 'Is she a friend of yours?'

Teo didn't have time to respond. The cleaner was coming towards the desk.

'I found this under the chair over there,' the older woman said, holding out a leather wallet.

'Oh, my goodness.' The receptionist took the wallet. 'Thank you so much. Someone's probably worried sick about this.' She opened the wallet. It had a pocket at the back for notes and slots for credit cards on the other side. In the middle was a plastic-covered pocket for a driver's licence. 'Zoe Harper,' she said in astonishment. 'Good thing *you're* here, Dr Tuala.'

'Is it?'

'Well, she's a friend of yours. You could take it back to her.'

'I could.' Teo's tone was confident. Surely there'd be something in the wallet that would have her address on it? He could drop it off on his way home. He would get to see Zoe again. Even better, he could find out whether she had some support at home in the form of a partner.

He held out his hand for the wallet. 'I'm on my way home right now,' he said. 'Consider it sorted.'

CHAPTER THREE

THE knock on the door couldn't have come at a worse time.

Zoe was sitting in the tiny living room of her terraced cottage in one of Sydney's older suburbs. Emma had been bathed and changed and had just started her final feed for the evening. And, for once, it was going well. Sucking on her bottle, she lay in the crook of Zoe's arm, staring up at her mother. The memories of the awful morning they'd had in that waiting room were finally beginning to ebb away.

Zoe couldn't help jumping at the sound of the knock. Nobody came visiting at this time of day.

Her first thought was that it could be James and she didn't want to see him. There'd been undeniable relief on both sides when they'd decided to call it quits on their relationship. James had generously gifted her his share of the hefty deposit they'd put down on this cottage.

'Consider it child support,' he'd suggested. 'That way, we can go our own ways with no hard feelings.'

The gesture had been very generous, considering that Zoe had inherited a piece of land from her grandmother that was probably worth a lot now. Not that she'd had a chance to think about what to do with it with everything else that was happening in her life.

Even worse than it being James, there was the faint possibility it could be one of her parents, given that she had finally written to them to inform them that they were grandparents. But she hadn't expected a reply to the letter, let alone a personal appearance. They would see the fact that she was unmarried with a baby as further evidence of the trouble she'd caused from the moment she'd been born. Besides, how many years had it been since her mother had even left the house?

Zoe didn't know because she hadn't been in contact with them since she'd come to Sydney at the age of eighteen to start her training as a paramedic. That had been nearly ten years ago.

The possibilities flashed through her head so fast, she had considered them both by the time the knocking stopped. Both were enough to make her feel incredibly tense. Emma was still staring up at her but her contented sucking had stopped. She jerked her head back and the teat of the bottle sprang free and sent a spray of milk onto Zoe's face. Emma's face was crumpling ominously as a second knock came. Louder and more commanding than the first.

Her heart sinking, Zoe got to her feet. Emma would be howling by the time she got to the door. If someone was going to try and sell her an encyclopaedia or something, it could very well be the final straw.

It wasn't James. It wasn't her father and, thank goodness, it wasn't her mother.

That it was Teo Tuala rendered Zoe completely speechless. He had something in his hand that he was holding out towards her.

'The cleaner found this in the waiting room,' he said. 'Good thing you had your driver's licence in it. Even better that it had your address on it too.'

'Good grief… I thought I'd left it in the car. I was going to go and look for it when I got Emma off to sleep.'

Which wouldn't be any time soon. Emma was rubbing her nose against Zoe's shoulder and her wails were increasing in strength.

'I was just feeding her.' Zoe couldn't help sounding defensive. 'She was perfectly happy a moment ago.'

'And I interrupted by pounding on the door. Sorry.'

Teo really did have the most glorious smile.

It radiated charm with a good helping of contrition this time.

'I'll get back to it, then.' Zoe had Emma in her arms. She also still had the bottle in her hand. She hesitated for a second, wondering how to take hold of the wallet. 'Would you mind putting it on the hall table?'

'Not at all.' Teo followed her in. He closed the door behind him. He looked around. 'Nice place,' he said. 'I love these cottages. I live in a modern apartment block but only because it's handy for the hospital. I've got a house in Samoa, right by the beach.'

'Oh...' Zoe had an instant image of a tropical paradise. 'Do you get back there often?'

'I go back for a week every couple of months. I like to help out at the local hospital as much as I can.' His smile had a wry curl. 'It used to be to see all my relatives as well but a whole bunch of them live over here now and the others all come to visit. I've got my favourite cousin and her brood arriving tomorrow.'

He had a voice that was just like his personality, Zoe thought. Deep and rich and warm. It was relaxing to listen to. Even Emma seemed to like it. She was still grizzling but the head rubbing was slower. Suddenly, the awkward thought in the back of her head that she would have to usher Teo out when he seemed happy to stay and talk just melted away.

'Would you like a coffee or something?' she asked. 'It's the least I can do to thank you for coming all this way with my wallet.'

'That would be great.'

'I'll just need to finish feeding Emma first.'

'No worries.' Teo followed her into the living area. There was only the one couch in here. Zoe sat on one end, feeling the tilt of the cushions as Teo took the other end. He was so big, it meant that they were sitting very close together. Zoe pushed the awareness away. She tipped Emma back and offered her the bottle again.

Emma pulled away from the teat, turning her head one way and then the other. Her face got steadily redder as she gathered strength to let Zoe know that this was not going to work.

'I could have a go at that, if you'd like.' Teo's tone said it didn't matter in the least if she didn't like the idea. 'Seeing as it was my fault her supper got interrupted.'

He was offering to rescue her again. Because he thought she was pathetic?

'That way, you could make the coffee.' She could see a hint of mischief in his smile now. 'I haven't had one since about nine o'clock this morning and I'm having serious caffeine withdrawal.'

Not only was he offering to help, he was making it seem like she was doing *him* a favour. And did it matter if he thought she was pathetic? Judging by the way he'd handled Emma that morning, Teo was more likely to be successful in getting her fed and settled for the night. And if Emma settled, she would have a good sleep and be easier to look after tomorrow. Zoe would get a good sleep herself. She stamped on the pride or the need to prove herself or what-ever it was preventing her from accepting her visitor's help.

'That would be great,' she said, deliberately echoing Teo's acceptance of her offer of coffee. She handed over her baby and then the bottle. 'How do you like your coffee?'

'Dash of milk and two sugars.'

Zoe grinned. 'Good to see a medical profes-sional setting such a healthy example.'

'My aunties think I'm fading away. They give me six sugars. I'm in a programme to wean my-self of the addiction.' The skin around the cor-ners of his eyes was crinkling into well-worn smile lines. 'Hello, my name is Teo Tuala and I'm a sugarholic.'

A snort of laughter escaped Zoe, which made Emma's head turn. She looked surprised enough to have forgotten why she was crying. Teo eased the teat of the bottle into her open mouth and she turned back, sucking vigorously and reach-ing up with her hands to help hold the bottle.

'That's the ticket,' Teo said approvingly. 'Good girl, Emma.'

It didn't take Zoe long to make the coffee but by the time she brought two steaming mugs back from the adjacent kitchen, Emma had finished her milk. Teo had her upright on his shoulder, and was rubbing her back. Seconds later, Emma burped loudly.

Zoe shook her head at the ease with which Teo was going through the routine.

'How do you know so much about babies?'

'I'm a paediatrician.' Teo grinned. 'There was a class or two about babies, as I recall. I might have even read a book.'

Zoe didn't return the smile. 'I'm a mother,' she said. 'And I've read every book there is. I can't handle Emma that well.'

'I'm Samoan,' Teo said, as if that explained everything.

Maybe it did. Maybe there was some cultural secret to knowing what to do with babies. If Zoe could find out what it was, it might be the answer to all her problems. Searching his face for a clue, she suddenly realised how long she had been staring at him. She sat down hurriedly, feeling herself blushing.

The way Zoe blushed was a dead give-away that something had emotional importance. The way she had been looking at him gave Teo a good clue as to what it was. She was lost in her position as a mother. She thought he might be able to help. There was a touch of desperation there that made him want to help. And maybe he *did* have the answer.

'I didn't come to Australia until I was eight or nine,' Teo said, his tone much more sober. 'In the islands, as soon as you're old enough, you get to carry around the little kids and feed the babies and so on. Everybody has lots of brothers and sisters, or, in my case, an unlimited number of cousins. Family is everything at home.'

Not just at home in the islands. Family was everything, end of story. For a mother to be going out to work wasn't the answer. Especially to a job like the one Zoe had. She was putting herself in danger out there. Maybe it was none of his business but if he could do anything to persuade her there might be another way to regain her self-confidence, he had to try.

He knew, far too well, just how bad it could be for a child to lose his or her mother.

'I think the secret is just learning to relax. Be confident that you're doing the right thing because you love them. That's all that really matters in the end.'

'I do love Emma.' Zoe was nodding. 'I *do*.' The last words were a whisper, almost as though she was talking to herself. Convincing herself?

Emma was a heavy, limp bundle on his chest now. 'I think she's asleep,' he told Zoe. 'Want me to put her down?'

She nodded. 'Would you mind? If I take her, she'll probably wake up again.'

'Show me where her bed is.'

Zoe led him further down the narrow hallway of the cottage. There was a bathroom at the end of the hallway and two bedrooms on either side before that. He could see a double bed in the room on the right. It had a smooth, white cover and some cushions arranged very symmetrically. The one on the left was beautifully decorated with a teddy-bear theme. The bassinette had a white cover as pristine as the one on the adult bed and Teo could see baby supplies and toys arranged with absolute precision all around him. It looked like an advertisement for the perfect baby's bedroom.

It didn't look as if anyone actually lived in it.

Zoe turned back the cover on the bassinette and he laid Emma down carefully, on her side. She pulled the cover back up and tucked the edges in carefully. She smoothed the wrinkles on the top, stood back and then bent down. Teo expected to see her kiss her baby goodnight but, instead, she gently stroked the wisps of hair that were curling on her forehead, patting them back to sit in line with the rest of her hair.

Teo was deep in thought as he went back to the living area. He could see it all around him now. The attention to detail. The effort for everything to be perfect. No wonder Zoe was finding it hard to bond with her baby and be relaxed in her role of a mother. She was attempting the impossible here.

He knew exactly how he could help her. He also knew it was going to take some careful persuasion.

'How did your session with John go?' he asked, as they sat down to drink their coffee.

'Good. He's happy that my being back at work is going well.' Zoe wouldn't meet his gaze and Teo knew why. They both knew how concerned John would be if he'd seen how distressed both Zoe and Emma had been that morning. That could well be the key but Teo needed a little time to think about it. He changed tack.

'You're an amazing housekeeper. I don't think I've ever seen a house that has a baby in it looking this clean and tidy.'

Zoe flashed him a sideways glance. 'Is it *too* tidy? I get the occasional visit from one of the outworkers at the mothering unit. I wouldn't want them to think I was OCD or anything.'

'They might think you employed a very efficient housekeeper.'

'As if! Paramedic salaries, especially when you're on maternity leave, don't run to flash housekeepers.'

'You do get some help, though, don't you?'

'What do you mean?' Zoe was eyeing him warily. She had the most amazing eyes, Teo realised. Quite a light green, but they had a circle of darker colour around the irises and tiny shards of gold that radiated out from the pupils like sun rays. He'd never seen anything quite like them.

The expression in her eyes was more than wary now. He could see a flash of fear. Did she think he was implying that she needed help? That social services might swoop in and remove her baby if she was deemed to be coping either so well it seemed pathological or not well enough? He might be getting into deeper waters than he'd intended to here.

Teo did what he always did when faced with something potentially stressful. He took a deep breath and consciously relaxed. That way, he could get a good look at the bigger picture.

'I meant a partner,' he said casually. 'Emma's dad?'

'Long gone,' Zoe told him. 'We were only casually dating when I got pregnant. It was a disaster, really. I thought I was safe being on the Pill and it was that "maybe it's time to go to bed to see if there's any real chemistry going on here" kind of sex.'

'And there wasn't? Any real chemistry?'

Zoe sighed. 'Not enough. We had a go of trying to make it work but it wasn't going to happen. He helped me buy this house in lieu of having to remember he was a father by paying years of child support and that was that. We shook hands and went our separate ways when I was about seven months pregnant.'

'And you haven't heard from him since?'

'No. I did have the horrible thought it might be him when I heard you knocking at the door, though, and it made me realise that I really don't want to see him again.'

Teo wasn't surprised. Didn't the man want to know if he'd had a son or a daughter? That everything had gone well? How could any man go off and pretend it had never happened? Babies were so precious. On some level it was satisfying to know that this James was out of Zoe's life. He wasn't good enough for her *or* Emma.

Somewhere, in the back of his head, was a buzz that suggested the idea of sex with Zoe would be a very attractive prospect. He needed to distract himself, fast. The last thing Zoe Harper needed was another casual relationship that would probably only serve to strengthen whatever barriers were in place to stop her bonding completely with her baby.

'What about family?' he asked. 'They must be thrilled to have Emma around.'

'No family,' was all that Zoe said.

Even if Teo couldn't recognise an untruth, the way the colour flooded Zoe's cheeks made it clear that this was another emotional minefield. The way her shoulders had hunched indicated a boundary that he had no trouble recognising.

But he could sense that this was it. The hub of the problem.

'You need a family,' he told Zoe. 'And it's very lucky that you've met me.'

'Sorry?'

'I have more family than any one person could ever need. You'd be most welcome to borrow it.'

Zoe's stare told him that she thought he was crazy but Teo wasn't deterred.

'I told you my cousin's coming to visit. Alisi. She's got a little girl—Kali—who's not much older than Emma. And a couple of older boys. We're having a family barbecue next weekend at Coogee beach. Come and join us.'

'Oh, no...I couldn't possibly.'

Teo pulled out the big guns. 'You know what?'

Zoe wasn't playing. She was setting her coffee cup down on the table with great care. She even turned it around until she was happy with the angle of the handle. Her lips were pressed together resolutely. She wasn't going to encourage him by saying no.

'I reckon John would think it was a great idea, too,' Teo said.

That made her look up. 'Why?'

'He's helping you through your PND, isn't he?'

'Yes.'

'A big part of getting through it is to do with being confident about being with your baby, wouldn't you say?'

'I guess.'

'You asked me how I knew what I was doing and I said it was because I was Samoan. If you came and spent an afternoon with my tribe you'd understand. You might find a new way of looking at things.'

He could see the moment that a ray of hope shone through the wariness and determination to keep to herself. The hope that there was a key out there to unlock a door and let her step into the place she really wanted to be.

Teo believed he had that key.

'I'll pick you up,' he said. 'And if you aren't enjoying yourself, I'll take you home again, I promise.'

Zoe was gnawing her bottom lip so hard it hurt.

The invitation was pulling her in opposite directions. She desperately wanted to go because, if Teo was so good with babies, imagine what she might learn by watching how the women handled their children?

But what if it just came naturally because they were Samoan? They'd look at her and think she was some kind of freak. A mother who didn't know how to love her baby. Teo might be embarrassed that he'd even suggested including her.

And why was he issuing the invitation? This was a family gathering and she was a total stranger. What could he possibly be getting out of this? He must know that she wasn't remotely interested in getting involved with any man. Interest in sex had been wiped from her life even before James had disappeared. She hadn't even been touched by a man with anything other than a medical procedure in mind for well over a year.

Except for when Teo had touched her shoulder in the waiting room that morning. And that had been simply a way of getting her attention. Connecting. A touch of friendship.

Was it possible that she could have this gentle giant of a man as a friend? Someone who accepted her PND as well as her baby as simply being a part of who she was at the moment? Someone who didn't judge her and find her a miserable failure?

He wasn't saying anything. He seemed to be enjoying the last of his coffee, just letting the invitation float there in the air between them.

Zoe had a flash of something like panic. If she didn't catch it, it might disappear and she would be left wondering if she'd lost the most important opportunity she might ever have.

'I…um… What would I need to bring?'

'Just you and Emma,' Teo said promptly. 'No food, please. My family could cater for an army.' His smile carried a warmth that enfolded Zoe completely. 'And whatever you do, don't eat any breakfast. My aunties will take one look at you and think you need a lot more meat on your bones.'

Zoe made a face. 'Are you kidding? I'm two dress sizes bigger than I was before Emma.'

Teo's smile left his lips but it was still there in his eyes. 'The Samoan way of thinking is different. I think you might like it.'

If Teo was a typical representative, Zoe was quite prepared to believe that. The bubble of hope inside her was growing. It was almost a trickle of excitement and that was something Zoe hadn't felt for anything other than her job in longer than she could remember.

'So you'll keep next Saturday free? You'll come to our barbecue?'

Zoe nodded shyly. 'Thank you. I'd love to.'

CHAPTER FOUR

IT WAS just as well Zoe hadn't needed to think about bringing food.

A beach outing with a baby was enough of a mission in itself. She had to pack a supply of clean nappies and wipes, bottles and premixed formula, sunscreen and hats and toys to entertain her with and two changes of clothes. The car seat could double as a place for Emma to take a nap but she had to find a muslin cloth that could provide shade and protection from insects.

April was the second month of autumn in Australia but there were still days that felt like summer and this was one of them. A clear, blue sky and not a breath of wind. The surf was picture perfect, rolling up the white sandy beach, but Teo didn't lead Zoe down the steps to the sand. He headed for the large grassed area dotted with trees and some permanent barbecue sites. Every one of them was being used today by groups of families and friends but Zoe could spot the gathering they were heading towards well before they got there.

It was the most crowded. The most colourful. And by far the noisiest. She could see women of generous proportions wearing brightly coloured floral dresses and men wearing board shorts and T-shirts like Teo was. And there were children. It seemed like there were dozens of children running around and the younger they got, the less in the way of clothing they were wearing. Two tots weren't even wearing nappies.

Zoe felt completely overdressed in her jeans and singlet top. She also felt intimidated by the shouting and laughter she could hear. And they were all Samoan people, which made her feel pale and out of place. Her steps slowed.

'I'm not at all sure about this,' she confessed. 'I had no idea your family was so big.'

Teo let her catch up. He was carrying Emma while Zoe had the overstuffed nappy bag. 'I wasn't expecting this many either,' he said. 'Word gets around the community, though, and I expect everybody wanted to welcome Alisi and the kids. Come on, I'll introduce you to Alisi. I think you two will get on just fine.'

Amazingly, they did. After a series of introductions that made Zoe's head swim and hugs that felt as warm and squashy as the most comfortable couch in the world from all the 'aunties', Zoe found herself sitting on the grass beside Teo's favourite cousin.

'I love your jeans,' Alisi said. 'You'll have to tell me where I can go shopping.'

'Bondi Junction's good.' Zoe unstrapped Emma and picked her up from the car seat. Far more effort had gone into dressing her daughter than herself and Emma was wearing a pretty, smocked pink dress, white socks and tiny sandals.

'Oh...isn't she gorgeous?' Alisi's face lit up with a wide smile that reminded Zoe of Teo's grin. She reached out to touch Emma's face with her forefinger. *'Lalelei pepe,'* she crooned.

Inexplicably, Zoe felt the prickle of tears at such effusive admiration of her baby. Emma *was* beautiful. She felt proud of her.

'Yours is a darling, too. Her name's Kali, yes?'

'Ai.' Alisi nodded. 'And those two ragamuffins plaguing Teo are my *ui*, Maru and Sefa.'

Teo didn't look like he was being plagued. He had half a dozen small boys in bright board shorts and nothing else dancing around him as he dribbled a football across the grass. There was a whoop of excitement when he kicked it and the boys competed hard to be the first to reach the ball. Except for one, who clung to Teo's hand.

'That's Sefa.' Alisi smiled. 'His uncle Teo is his favourite person in the world.'

Alisi's baby was enjoying a breastfeed. All Zoe could see were chubby brown limbs and nothing more than a singlet and nappy for clothing. Emma was even more overdressed for this outing than she herself was. In an attempt to cover her sudden awkwardness, she found a bottle of sunscreen and began smoothing it over her daughter's equally chubby limbs.

She was fitting a frilled, white sunhat on her head when one of the aunties spotted Emma.

'Oh…' she cried. 'The *lalelei pepe*. Please…' She held out her arms and Zoe didn't have time to even consider refusing to share her child. Emma was scooped into strong brown arms and carried away to be shown off. Zoe watched in astonishment as Emma was passed from one woman to another, often after what was obviously a difference in opinion over how long someone's turn should be. What was even more astonishing was that Emma seemed to be loving it.

Teo must have been keeping half an eye on

her while playing football with the boys. Maybe he could sense her astonishment and took it for concern because he eventually called in one of his cousins to take over supervising the children and went to rescue Emma. He plucked her from the arms of a woman who had the most beautiful long black hair and a frangipangi bloom tucked behind an ear.

'My turn,' Zoe heard him say with authority. 'I'm her honorary uncle, after all.'

He held Emma with his two huge hands around her middle. Zoe's breath caught in horror as he suddenly swooped her skywards so that she was balanced in his hands looking down at his head. Then he bounced her. Emma's face split into the biggest grin ever and the gurgling sound of her laughter could be clearly heard.

Everybody watching beamed approvingly.

'*Ua fiafia le teine.*' Alisi smiled. 'She's happy.'

And Zoe wanted to cry. It was the first time she had heard her baby laugh.

Teo brought Emma back to her then.

'Don't know about her,' he said, 'but I'm starving. I'll help with the cooking and then it's time for a swim.'

Zoe found a bottle of formula and Emma didn't object to having cold milk. She saw Alisi glance at the bottle and cringed inwardly but she couldn't detect the slightest judgement in the glance. In fact, Alisi sighed with something that sounded like envy.

'Her hair is so lovely. Like the first kiss of sunset. We get the most beautiful sunsets in the world in the islands.'

'I'll bet.'

'Have you ever been to Samoa?'

'No. I've never been out of Australia.'

'You'll have to come and visit.' The statement held as much authority as Teo's had when he'd reclaimed Emma and announced his position as her honorary uncle.

Did he mean that? Would that make him an honorary cousin for her? Someone with the kind of bond that was palpable amongst this big group of happy people? The notion was more than appealing. It gave Zoe an ache of longing. She'd never had any siblings. Or cousins. Or even a family in the true sense of the word.

'We would love to have you,' Alisi added. And then she laughed. 'My husband, Rangi, refuses to leave the islands. He expects the world to come to him. I said I had to go and visit Teo and he couldn't understand why. Teo comes here every few weeks, he said. Why go all that way to a smelly city?'

'Does he? Go home every few weeks?'

'He has a house near the beach. He says it's the home of his heart. He works for a week at the local hospital at least once every three months or so.'

'Really?' Zoe was impressed. 'That's a wonderful thing for him to do.'

Alisi nodded. 'Everybody loves Teo. He has the respect of a chief.'

The two young women were sitting on a rug beneath the shade of one of the trees close to the barbecue area. Everyone else seemed to have something to do around them, either playing with the children or preparing the food. Delicious aromas of garlic and lemon, seafood and roasting meat were drifting over the area, bringing the children to crowd around the picnic tables.

Zoe found herself watching Teo. There was a lot of laughter happening around the hot grills of the barbecues, the group of men clearly good friends.

'How many of you are Teo's family?' she asked.

Alisi laughed again. She had her baby lying in her lap now and she was holding Kali's hands, gently making her dance with her arms.

'All of us,' she said. 'And none of us, in a way.'

'What do you mean?'

'Teo was an only child. His father died in a fishing accident when he was a tiny baby. His mother met an Australian tourist and came here to be with him but she was sick and didn't realise it. By the time they found the cancer it was too late to treat it. I think that's why Teo works at our hospital so often. He doesn't want that to happen to anybody else. Anyway, her man left her and she was too ashamed to come back home. Teo cared for her and he was too young to know how to come home when she died. He ended up in foster-care until Hina found him one day, in trouble on the streets. He was about thirteen then.'

'Hina?'

'Over there. In the blue and white *lavalava*. Sarong, I mean. She took him into her family. Adopted him, in the end, because there were a lot of papers to sign. That wouldn't happen in the islands. Our families can be blended without any of that fuss. Anyway, she's his first auntie and she has a lot of family here.'

Zoe was curious now. To be alone as a child and watch his mother die of cancer would have been appalling. And Alisi's tone when she'd mentioned foster-care had been one of enough disgust to suggest that the care hadn't been acceptable. Something clicked in the back of her head. No wonder he was prepared to bend rules and keep children in hospital with their mothers if the alternative was a foster-care system he didn't trust.

Something else shone through as well. Teo had been found in trouble. On the streets. How awful had that time been for him? And how could someone end up radiating the generosity of spirit and laid-back charm that Teo had if he'd had such an unhappy childhood?

He was the most extraordinary man.

Emma had finished her lunch as everybody else began eating what was, to Zoe, the most extraordinary feast. The aunties insisted on cuddling both Emma and Kali, clearly well practised in juggling babies and eating their meals one-handed. Alisi was happy to hand Kali over and Zoe felt relaxed enough by now to do the same with Emma.

'You've got to try this,' Alisi said, reaching

for a huge, plastic bowl on the table. 'It's called *okai'a*. It's lime-marinated tuna. Delicious. Sefa! Put that back. You only need *one* coconut bun.'

'And this is my favourite.' Teo appeared by Zoe's side, and put some meat fresh from the grill onto her plate. 'Honey-glazed chicken.'

'Thank you. It smells wonderful.'

He hesitated for a moment. 'You OK?' he asked quietly. 'Enjoying yourself?'

Zoe nodded. 'They're very kind people.'

'You coming for a swim later?'

Zoe shook her head this time. 'I didn't bring my bathing suit.'

'I could lend you a sarong,' Alisi offered. 'No good for swimming but we could take the babies paddling.'

'Great idea,' Teo said. 'When the tide goes out a bit further, there'll be some lovely shallow pools down there near the swimming pool.'

The rock pool was set into the cliff side and was large enough for any swimmers who wanted to stay out of the surf. At high tide, the waves broke over the edge of the pool but it was far enough out now for the pool to look as clear and calm as a mountain lake. Inviting enough for Zoe to wish she had brought her bathing suit. It had occurred to her to do so but the new curves of her post-pregnancy body were not something she had any desire to put on display. Anywhere. Her concerns seemed a bit silly now, in the company of so many women who were obviously completely at ease with their larger figures.

There were platters of fresh fruit offered for dessert and a taro bread pudding that Hina had made. And then, by tacit consent, the whole group settled for a rest period. Someone produced a guitar and started singing softly. Several small children went to sleep on the laps of adults, including Emma, who was tucked into the folds of Hina's blue and white sarong. When Zoe offered to take her back to put her in her car seat, Hina waved her away with a smile.

So Zoe sat with Alisi in the shade of the tree, listening to the music and watching the waves breaking on the beach and the crowd of people out enjoying the gorgeous day. Coogee beach was a very popular place on a day like this and Zoe wouldn't have been surprised if she knew some of the people out there, swimming and sunbathing, but she had no desire to move away from this group of Teo's people.

She might be overdressed and the only pale person amongst them but somehow, in a very short space of time, they had made her feel as if she belonged.

The rest period appeared to be over with the same kind of unspoken agreement with which it had begun. Children woke up. Some of the women began clearing the table. Teo stood up and stretched.

'Time for a swim,' he announced. He stripped off his T-shirt, rolled it into a ball and threw it like a football to one of Alisi's sons.

'But I want to swim *with* you, Uncle Teo.'

'Later. I'm going out past the waves. Too deep for you, Sefa.' He turned away to head for the beach and Zoe caught her breath.

Teo's left arm, from above the elbow to the top of his shoulder, was covered with an intricate tattoo. The skin was almost black. It was the lines of uninked skin that made the patterns.

Alisi had noticed her involuntary gasp.

'Nice, isn't it?' she murmured.

Zoe didn't know what to say. Tattoos were not something she had ever associated with the kind of man she knew Teo to be.

Alisi smiled. 'It's a *pe'a*,' she told Zoe. 'Tattoo in Samoa is an art form. It's been practised for two thousand years. Originally, it was only meant for women of rank but now it's become a mark of manhood.'

It was certainly masculine. Zoe couldn't her take her eyes off Teo. She watched him run towards the surf, splash through the shallows and dive through a bigger wave. And then he was swimming, parallel to the shore, with a powerful overarm stroke that made his body move at an impressive speed.

She was still watching as he came out of the water and she was close enough to see the water dripping from the thick waves of his hair. The way his big, brown body glistened and the wet board shorts clung, leaving very little to the imagination.

The tribal tattoo *was* a work of art, she realised. As much a part of Teo as the rest of his rich, vibrant culture. And it was ultimately masculine. The mark of a warrior.

And from somewhere so deep within Zoe it took some moments to recognise what it was came the unfurling of physical desire.

An attraction more powerful than anything she had ever experienced. Or was it just because she'd been totally incapable of feeling the slightest interest in men since her life had been turned upside down by her pregnancy and then the depression?

Maybe it had something to do with the feeling of belonging to this group of people. This extended family. And it was more to do with something waking up inside her. A joyful thing that had not only been buried under the hopelessness of depression but had never really been there in the first place.

It wasn't as if it could go anywhere. This wasn't even any kind of a date, Zoe reminded herself, trying to drag her gaze away from Teo as he strode steadily closer and her heart rate picked up noticeably. He had offered to let her borrow his family, nothing more than that. Distraction was probably needed here.

'I think I'll take you up on that offer of the sarong,' she said to Alisi. 'I'd love to see what Emma thinks of getting her feet wet.'

The swim had been both relaxing and energising but it always left Teo with a poignant sense of homesickness.

He had seawater in his blood but it was never the same here. The water was so much colder and the surf wilder. The lagoons and gentle, sometimes barely there, waves of his boyhood beaches were central to his happiest memories of a time when life had been perfect.

When his mother had still been there, happy and healthy and waiting to enfold him in her love whenever life was difficult to cope with. His closest family. His strength.

Teo shook the sadness off, along with more water from his hair. He caught drips on his chin with his tongue and tasted the salt. At least he could get to the sea here. Finn Kennedy swam every day in a pool near the Kirribilli View apartments. He had invited Teo to join him more than once but for Teo, swimming in such an artificial environment would be soul destroying. Pools were akin to growing bonsai trees or something. A kind of travesty of the real thing.

The pools built into the sides of the cliffs along this coastline were different. The edges were carved from the same wild rocks that surrounded the manmade area. The waves filled them and kept them fresh and clear and salty. He could see people in the closest pool with their young children, teaching them to swim. The tide was well out now, exposing other rocks down on the sand and filling hollows to make shallow pools that would be warm from the sun.

He could also see Zoe and Alisi down there with their babies. Zoe had changed into a *lava-lava*. She had it knotted just above her breasts and had tucked the ends up into her knickers. Her legs were long and pale and…very eye catching. Teo caught himself smiling. Good grief…was he feeling attracted to Zoe? That wouldn't do at all, considering he'd offered her a family outing as nothing more than a friend. Maybe his pleasure in watching her was simply because his idea had been so successful. It looked as though Zoe and his favourite cousin were becoming fast friends and, while she had looked a bit tense and shy to start with today, she was certainly far more relaxed now.

Emma was wearing her sunhat but nothing

else. Little Kali was completely naked. Zoe seemed to be following Alisi's example, holding Emma upright under her arms and letting her feet catch the very last curl of surf as the long, low waves rolled in. He heard the shriek of an excited baby and the soft sound of feminine laughter and both the sight of the women and the sound of their pleasure was another nostalgic tug.

'Come on, Sefa. Maru? You want to come for a paddle?'

'Yes! Piggyback, Uncle Teo,' demanded Maru.

'Me too! Me too!' cried Sefa.

Teo grinned. *'E leai se popole.* No worries. You can both climb on board.'

He took both small boys out into deeper water and made his body into a raft for them to cling to. Maru, at four years old, could already swim like a little fish in calm water but he wasn't ready for the kind of rogue wave Coogee could throw in. Or the rips that lurked like an undersea monster, waiting to drag people away. Sefa was only two and Teo kept an arm loosely around the small, brown body at all times. There was a lot of splashing and laughter and Teo knew that both Alisi and Zoe were watching them.

And he liked that. He especially liked that Zoe was watching him. It could have contributed to how short the swim with the boys was because when he led them out of the waves, with one small hand in each of his, he took them to where the women were, in the rocks that extended out from the walls of the pool.

The tide was on the way back in now. Soon it would be time to pack up and head home but there were more moments of pleasure to be found. Like this one, where Alisi and Zoe were sitting beside the rocks with their babies on the sand beside them. They were protected by the rocks but these were wild rocks and there was no concrete to fill the gaps. When the waves came in and curled up against the barrier, there were gaps that let the sea water through, like fat hoses being turned on. The small, new waves rushed over the sand where they all sat, soaking sarongs and foaming over fat little baby legs.

Kali was giggling every time. So was Emma. And there was the occasional shriek of laughter if the gap between the waves was a little longer than the one before. Emma and Kali would look at each other while they were waiting and grin. Zoe looked up at Teo and smiled.

It was the first *real* smile he had seen her give. One that reached those astonishing green eyes and lit her whole face up with joy. She was loving this time with her baby. Loving being alive.

The idea that he'd found two such different personalities in the same woman had intrigued him. He'd seen the competent professional paramedic and the scared, lonely young mother. This was a third personality. Someone joyful and vibrant and…absolutely gorgeous.

Teo could feel a bubble of something warm and soft getting bigger in his chest. A combination of nostalgia and longing and…*hope*?

Whatever it was, it was cut off abruptly by the scream of a child in pain.

'*Sefa.*'

The small boy had been happily climbing over the rocks surrounding Alisi and Zoe but now he was hunched into a ball, shrieking with agony. His foot was covered in blood. Teo scooped him up and ran to deeper water to wash the blood away so that he could see what he was dealing with. A stubbed toe, probably.

It was. But it was such a bad stub that the big toenail had been almost ripped off. Teo knew that the best thing to do would be to get it off completely. He also knew it would hurt. He loved this little boy. The thought of hurting him made him feel sick.

Lessons well learned from the past were there to draw on. You couldn't help the people you loved if you couldn't keep enough distance to remain professional. Yes, it would hurt to rip the nail off but only for a split second. If he gave in to what his heart told him instead of his brain,

Sefa would be in pain for hours and then have the terror of a doctor's surgery or the ED and the pain of a local anaesthetic that would be just as bad as what he was about to do.

Because he had to.

Teo waited for the next wave, so he could hold Sefa's foot under the cold, rushing water. He took a good grip on the edge of the toenail.

'Sorry, buddy,' he murmured.

And then it was done. The sea water cleaned the wound and Sefa had stopped sobbing by the time he carried the child back to his mother. He clung to Teo, his head buried against his shoulder, and even his whimpers had almost stopped by the time he reached Alisi.

'His toenail had to come off,' he explained. 'I did it then, rather than making him wait. We need to dress it but it'll stop hurting soon.'

Alisi nodded, gathering her youngest son into her arms. Teo picked up Kali for her. He could sense that Zoe was watching him carefully. Maybe she thought it was cruel that he hadn't waited until the toe could be anaesthetised to make the procedure painless.

He didn't want to talk about it.

'I think it might be time to go home,' he said. When he looked up, Zoe wasn't watching him any longer. She was wrapping Emma in a towel.

'Yes,' she said, without turning her head. 'I think it is.'

CHAPTER FIVE

THE knocking had started.

Sharply staccato. A sound that came from nowhere in the dark and Finn Kennedy knew there was no escape.

He was trapped.

The nightmare was here yet again.

It always began like this. The crescendo of knocking that was the sound of anti-aircraft fire. The blessed darkness that deep sleep brought was punctured by streaks of bright, white light. The red fireball of a mortally wounded fighter jet spiralling down from on high was merely a background because now the buildings of the army base were shaking. The ground was shaking.

He had to find Isaac.

His younger brother was here somewhere in the army base. The all-consuming urgency with which he had to find and protect his brother was bone deep, honed by so many years of watching out for the only person he truly loved as they'd survived a childhood and adolescence of care homes and trouble.

Thank goodness he was here now. Becoming one of the stooped figures running through the base as the bombs exploded and shrapnel ricocheted from every direction. Finn knew it was only by chance he could save Isaac. This was his last tour of duty and he would soon be a civilian. Safe. Free to follow his dreams of medicine that wasn't being practised in a war zone.

The nightmare had the cruellest twists, however. Even as he ran now, with the desperate hope of finding Isaac and keeping him safe, he knew that at any moment he would become a victim himself. The blow on his head that was coming would knock him out briefly. The pain from the shrapnel in his body would almost in-capacitate him when he regained consciousness.

That wasn't the worst layer of awareness, though. At an even deeper level he also knew that he would get through that pain and fear and be able to struggle on.

To find Isaac.

To hold his beloved brother in his arms as he died.

The grief would always wake him. In sleep, as in life, he could never get past that moment when his ability to feel any kind of emotion died along with Isaac.

Waking never ended the nightmare com-pletely either. The layers were all still there in his head. The sounds and sights and smells. The fear. The grief. They swirled and tormented and there was only one way to try and escape.

An agonised groan escaped Finn as he raised his head from his hands. Throwing the covers off and swinging his legs so he was sitting on the side of his bed was so automatic he hadn't even been aware of the movement. Looking at his bedside clock was always the next step but it was only 3 a.m.

Far too early to go swimming and wash away the remnants of the nightmare with the combination of gruelling exercise and clean, cold water.

But neither could he stay in the confines of this apartment where the nightmare still filled the air and made him feel like he was breathing treacle. Just as well he had a plan B. One that he had used before with good effect.

Kirribilli View apartments had fire-escape stairs. A narrow column on a corner of the building. Flight after flight of bare, concrete steps, lit well enough on each landing to ensure people wouldn't fall and break their necks.

Nobody else used this access by preference, especially at 3 a.m. It was there for emergencies. And nobody else would be crazy enough to run down from the penthouse to the ground-floor exit, turn and take the steps two at a time to get back to the top. A minute or less to catch his breath and he could do it again.

And again.

It always took a while because it wasn't just a matter of shoving the memories dredged up by the nightmare back where they belonged. All the negative effects of the tragedy that had coloured the last ten years of his life tended to surface as well. It was a process that was becoming a habit. The self-recrimination for things he did. The justification for them. They never changed. Finn had learned to live with them.

The first run up and down the unforgiving steps—like the first few laps of the pool— were about burying the bombing raid that had killed Isaac. The second run was always about Lydia—Isaac's wife. The only link left to his brother. The self-recrimination was that he'd used that link. He'd used Lydia until she'd been strong enough to break off their half-hearted relationship.

You only want me because I remind you of

Isaac. I need to move on, Finn. I need to start living again.

He'd used a lot of women since Lydia. Who knew why they found him attractive? But he took advantage of that when he needed a reprieve from being so alone. When he needed the release that only sex could bring.

He couldn't even remember all of their names. That recrimination took care of the next uphill slog. Finn was tiring now. Mariette had been a couple of months ago and she'd been happy to break up with him, moving on to better things with that young paediatric doctor. The latest one hadn't been so happy. He'd only broken that off last week and there'd been tears. He'd been unkind to her but he just couldn't stand tears. Such a visible display of weakness. What was he supposed to do about them? Feel sorry for what he'd done or said? Sympathetic for the way someone else felt? Not going to happen. *Couldn't* happen.

Even with Evie?

The rebellious whisper in the back of his head was easy to dismiss. *Especially* with Evie.

Personal relationships of any kind were unacceptable. His interactions with people were based on science and you could only do the greatest good for the greatest number by shutting out the annoying influence of emotional complications.

Finn needed to catch his breath before he reached the top this time. Concrete wasn't a good surface to run on. It jarred his neck and the pain was starting to bite now, radiating into his shoulder. That was good. This was the point he always needed to get to because physical pain was infinitely preferable to mental distress. He'd pushed himself so hard this time he couldn't make it back to the top. He actually needed to lean against the wall for support.

It was then he heard the sound of footsteps approaching from below.

Who the hell would be coming into the apartments at this time of night? By this stairwell?

Teo Tuala, that's who.

'Hey…' To his credit, Teo didn't sound at all disturbed by the sight of Sydney Harbour Hospital's director of surgery in an unlikely place, completely out of breath, at 4 a.m. 'Did you get called in for that nasty MVA, too?'

Wearing his running shorts and an ancient T-shirt? Hardly likely he'd head out looking like this. Still, it was an easy excuse to use.

'I'll go in soon. I was just getting my exercise out of the way.' Finn knew he sounded out of breath. Teo might be looking as laid back as he always did but there was something about the way he was watching Finn right now that made him feel uncomfortable. Breaking eye contact, he tilted his head and rubbed at the back of his neck, turning to make his way up to the next landing.

'Me, too.' Teo was following him. 'I've taken a pledge to use the stairs instead of the lifts.'

When they reached the landing, Teo got to the

fire stop door first. He held it open. 'You OK?' he asked quietly.

Finn gave him the look anybody got if they asked a personal question like that but Teo didn't seem cowed.

'You look a bit sore, that's all,' he said. 'You were rubbing your neck a minute ago and now it's your arm.'

God…it was becoming a habit. Maybe he needed to bump up the painkillers.

'It's nothing,' he said dismissively.

'Old war wound?'

'Something like that.' Finn turned away sharply enough to twist something that made him wince. He walked away. 'It's nothing,' he snapped again. 'Get some sleep, Teo. You'll need it if you want to be on top of your game tomorrow.'

'You look like you had a hard night.'

'Yeah…' Teo pushed the button that controlled the pedestrian crossing on this main intersection. 'I should have been a psychologist, shouldn't I?'

'There's certainly something to be said for a nine-to-five job.' John Allen's smile for his neighbour was sympathetic. 'Hope it wasn't anything too traumatic that kept you up.'

'Car crash at midnight. Pregnant woman and three kids involved. Woman ended up going into labour so I hung around to make sure the baby was OK.'

'Was it?'

'Fortunately, yes. Few weeks prem but he should be fine. Hey…Luke…' He turned to greet the man who'd joined them. 'Did you get any sleep?'

'Not enough.'

He didn't look too bothered by it but Luke didn't look bothered by much these days. Still on cloud nine, obviously, thanks to the effects of being so much in love with Lily. Teo didn't see either of them much these days. They stayed out on Luke's farm unless the traffic was too awful or Luke was kept too late, as he had been last night.

The buzzing sound and green signal to cross propelled the men into movement. 'What time did you get in?' John asked Teo.

''Bout 4 a.m. Would you believe I found Finn Kennedy on the fire escape stairs? Looked like he'd been doing a circuit class or something.'

'He likes keeping fit.'

'I like keeping fit, too, but not at that time of night.'

They walked in silence for half a block. The grey sky seemed to be pressing down on Teo and if it rained, it would get cold. Not like in the islands. Alisi had gone home again yesterday and had made him promise to persuade Zoe to go to Samoa for a visit. Would John think that was a good idea? Should he even be talking to a colleague about a patient he had a personal interest in? Certainly not when Luke was there, even if he was a good mate. The interest he had in John's patient was confusing enough, without helpful mates pushing him in a direction he knew it would be unwise to go.

He'd had other things on his mind this morning, anyway.

'What is it with Finn?' he found himself asking. 'How can he handle his patients so well when his interpersonal relationships with everybody else are so bad?'

'You want a professional opinion?'

'Absolutely.'

John grinned. 'I think he has issues.'

'Hey…I could have told *you* that and I'm just a paediatrician.'

'I could have told you that, too,' Luke put in. 'He walked out in the middle of surgery a few weeks ago and left me to carry on. And Evie said something, too.'

'Oh?' Teo was well distracted from thinking about Zoe now and that had to be a good thing. Maybe he was going to find out what that odd undercurrent he'd sensed in Emergency between Finn and Evie was all about.

'She was worried about him.'

'Evie doesn't strike me as a worrying type,' John put in.

'No. That's what I thought, too.'

'What did she say?'

'She had some story about him dropping a clipboard. His hand being shaky. I wasn't listening that carefully, I have to admit. I had something else on my mind.'

'I'll bet.' Teo knew exactly what that 'something else' had probably been—a very attractive, blue-eyed blonde nurse by the name of Lily Ellis.

'She seemed to think we were more than drinking buddies but Finn doesn't let anybody that close, does he?'

'No.' The agreement from the other men was heartfelt.

'He certainly shut me out pretty fast last night,' Teo added.

'I didn't do anything about it,' Luke said. 'Maybe I should have.'

'Maybe you hit the nail on the head by saying you were drinking buddies,' Teo suggested. 'We all know he drinks a lot. Everybody who goes to Pete's knows how hard he can hit the whisky at times. The question is, why?'

'PTSD?' Luke offered.

Both Luke and Teo glanced at John but the psychologist only shrugged.

'He's never talked to me. I doubt that he'd be willing to talk to anyone.'

'No...' Teo could feel himself frowning. 'He looked like he was in pain last night but he wouldn't tell me anything. According to the grapevine, he got injured quite badly just before he left his army post.'

'A grapevine? At the Harbour?' John was grinning again. 'No-o...'

'His last conquest was a paediatric nurse,' Teo told him. 'I found her sobbing in the sluice room and had to hear all about it. Seems she's the latest in a long string of heartbroken females who find our director of surgery very appealing, despite the fact that he's so grumpy and never seems to bother shaving.'

'Very macho.'

'It's no wonder they call our place of work Sydney Scandal Central.' Luke grinned.

Teo chuckled. 'And what's the deal between him and Evie Lockheart?'

'What do you mean?'

'I saw them talking to each other in ED last week and I got the oddest impression that there was something going on. Something personal that didn't fit with what I've heard about the scraps they have.'

'Maybe it's familiar territory for her,' John mused. 'Not that I'm one to gossip but it's common knowledge that she had to battle her father to be able to do medicine in the first place and Richard Lockheart can be a difficult character, by all accounts.'

'Maybe she's attracted to a father figure.' Teo regretted the quip as soon as it left his lips. It was none of his business whether there was any kind of potential relationship going on between a pair of the Harbour's better-known staff members. He didn't want to go down the track of discussing such a possibility, either, because if he did, he might be steered into considering a far more personal attraction that was creating ripples in his own life right now. Good grief…he just couldn't stop thinking about Zoe for more than five minutes, could he?

'If Finn Kennedy's her choice, then good luck to her,' John said.

'Professional opinion?' Another joke seemed a good way to lighten the sudden tension Teo was aware of.

'Could be the making of the man,' Luke said, with the slightly smug air of a man who'd found exactly what he hadn't even been looking for.

'Of course.' But John didn't seem to be paying any real attention to the conversation now. He was looking beyond Teo. Towards an apartment block that was far older and more rundown than the Kirribilli View apartments.

'Oh, my God!' he said, the tone of dismay increasing with each word. 'Is that *smoke*?'

CHAPTER SIX

SYDNEY'S Kangaroo Day Care centre was one of the best.

The facility catered for babies and children aged from six weeks to five years and it had a great carer to child ratio. Zoe had never had the slightest qualms about leaving Emma there. It had, in fact, been a relief to start handing her child over on a regular basis when she'd gone back to part-time work. It meant that Emma was frequently in the care of these devoted professionals who knew far more about it all than she did. Not only did she get a reprieve from the difficult task of being a single parent, she got to go back to her old job for a good stretch of time. Back to being the old Zoe.

But something had changed.

Today, as she'd left Emma in another woman's arms and turned to leave, she'd felt a distinct qualm.

A small niggle, maybe, but enough for Zoe to turn and take another look at her daughter before going out through the rainbow-painted doors of the day-care centre with their round porthole windows.

It was guilt, she decided, driving towards the start of her shift at the Harbourside ambulance station. It wasn't as if Emma was crying or anything. On the contrary, she'd been smiling at the woman giving her a cuddle. And that background buzz of guilt should be something that Zoe was more than used to by now.

She'd felt guilty about getting pregnant in the first place. How stupid had she been to let that happen in this day and age? She felt even more guilty for considering the option of terminating the pregnancy but, most of all, she'd felt guilty for not feeling the way a mother should feel when her baby was born.

For not loving her child with all her heart and soul.

So, yes…Zoe was used to feeling guilty. So why did that pang on leaving Emma behind this morning feel different somehow?

Not that she wanted to waste time at work pondering something that was no part of her professional life but the day started by conspiring against her. It was unusually quiet and Tom wanted to chat as they went through the normal routine of making sure their ambulance was fully equipped and operational.

'We need more lancets for the blood glucose kit,' he noted. 'Did you have a good weekend?'

'It was great.'

'What'd you get up to?'

'I got invited to a barbecue at Coogee.'

'Nice weather for it.'

'It was. Fabulous.' Zoe went to the storeroom to get a handful of the tiny plastic devices that held needles for pricking fingers and testing drops of blood for sugar levels.

It *had* been a fabulous day, even though it had ended on a vaguely disturbing note with poor little Sefa having that toe-stubbing incident. Teo had seemed slightly distant on the way home, too. Still perfectly relaxed and friendly but Zoe had had the definite impression that a shutter or two had gone up. The horrible thought occurred to her that he might have somehow sensed her attraction to him and was letting her know that it was pointless. The thought was enough to ensure that she probably seemed equally distant.

In any case, it couldn't spoil what the day had given her. She'd heard her baby laugh for the first time. Such an amazing sound of undiluted joy—as if it didn't matter how hard Zoe was finding it to be a parent or that Emma was missing out on what every other mother seemed to be able to give their child naturally. It was impossible to hear the sound of baby laughter and not feel an echo of that joy yourself. And it was an echo that had stayed with her for the few days until she'd been rostered back on at work. The last of it had probably only gone this morning, when she'd had that odd qualm.

Even now, when she remembered Emma smiling at the woman from Kangaroo's, the qualm came back. Maybe it had something to do with the fact that it was someone else that Emma was smiling at, not her. Jealousy?

How ridiculous. Her baby had beamed at everyone on the day of the barbecue. She'd even giggled when Alisi had been tickling her toes the day the two women had gone shopping for jeans at Bondi Junction together. She hadn't felt jealous then. She'd felt…good grief…*happy*?

She was happy now, Zoe reminded herself firmly. At work. Able to do the things she'd trained so hard to be able to do. She had the next twelve hours to be professional. Ready for anything. In control.

A mental note was called for here, Zoe decided as she turned her attention to making good use of their quiet time by cleaning the ambulance thoroughly. Heavens…look at the way dust could accumulate so fast around the regulators on the big oxygen cylinders.

Yes. She made a note to tell John Allen in her next session how well everything was going. She could tell him with absolute honesty that she was experiencing moments of real happiness again for the first time since this whole nightmare had started. That she could see light at the end of the tunnel and knew that, one day, she would be well again.

She wouldn't tell him about that confusing little qualm, though. Zoe didn't want anybody telling her that the road to happiness lay with being a mother and not getting back to being the person she'd been before she'd got pregnant. She couldn't be a full-time mother. She'd just get sucked back into that dark place and it would be far, far worse for Emma than being left in the lovely, caring environment of Kangaroo Day Care.

Zoe stopped wiping and polishing surfaces and decided to take out all of the towels from their locker and refold them. She was saved from this mindless task, however, by the sound of her pager. She'd only started reading the message when Tom appeared at a run.

'Local job,' he called. 'Standby for the fire service. There's an apartment block on fire.'

It was her turn to drive. Zoe slid into the seat, pushed the remote to open the huge roller door to the station and started the engine. She activated the beacons as they cleared the door and hit the siren as soon as she turned onto the road.

No qualms now. This might not be a moment of pure joy but the satisfaction of heading towards a challenging job was just as good. Better, in fact, because she'd know exactly what to do when she got there.

There were still people trapped.

Three fire engines were on site now and there were police cordoning off streets, controlling traffic and bystanders. A police helicopter was hovering overhead as well, or was it a news crew filming the incident? It wouldn't be a rescue chopper because they were so close to the Harbour. There were ambulances here anyway, off to one side and well away from the danger of smoke inhalation or falling debris.

Was Zoe here? Part of Teo hoped she was because he wanted to see her again but a bigger part of him hoped she was safely at home. With Emma. Teo headed in the direction of the burning apartment block anyway, in case extra medical assistance was needed. Luke was beside him and had almost tripped on a coil of black hose unfurling beside a fire truck.

'Watch out for the hoses.'

Teo could only nod. If he tried to say anything, he'd start coughing again.

It had been John who'd alerted the emergency services when he'd spotted smoke curling from a window on one of the building's upper floors. Teo and Luke had rushed into the apartment block, going in different directions to bang on doors and yell to raise the alarm.

Teo had been driven by something like fury when he'd run upstairs to the second floor. The building might be too old and rundown to have any kind of sprinkler system but there was no excuse for it not to have smoke detectors and an efficient alarm sounding to warn goodness only knew how many people who needed to escape.

He'd sent a young mother and her pyjama-clad children running downstairs to safety. Then he'd found some foreign students who were confused and frightened but could at least get out by themselves. The elderly man he'd come across next had needed help to get down the stairs. Teo had turned back to get to the third floor but he couldn't get very far. There was smoke billowing down the staircase by now and he could hear the crackle of flames from above and Luke yelling from below.

'The fire service is here. They're getting ladders to the top floors. They said to get out.' He could hear Luke coughing harshly. '*Now*, Teo.'

Teo had no choice. He'd covered his mouth

and nose with his arm but he could already feel the smoke biting into his lungs and his eyes were stinging. He passed firemen wearing breathing apparatus and carrying axes as he made his way outside. The right people were on the job now. He'd done all he could inside.

They might be needed outside, anyway. The area around the ambulances was busy.

And Zoe *was* here. In charge of the scene. Why did that surprise him when she'd been wearing that scene commander's vest the first time he'd seen her? Maybe it was because he'd met the other Zoes since then. The unhappy young mother. The beautiful young woman wearing a sarong on the beach…

'We'll treat it as cardiac,' he heard her saying to another paramedic. 'Usual protocol and transport immediately.'

The elderly man he'd helped down the stairs was on a stretcher, clearly short of breath. He had an oxygen mask on his face and the leads from a life pack attached to his chest. They were about to load him into one of the ambulances but he saw Teo and stretched out his hand. He pulled his oxygen mask off with his other hand.

'Thank you,' he croaked. 'Wouldn't have… got out…without you.'

'No worries.' Teo grasped the man's hand and smiled. He could feel Zoe pause and turn to stare.

'Teo! What are you doing here?'

'I was on my way to work. We spotted the fire.'

'And you went *inside*?'

'He got me out,' the elderly man said. 'Carried me…down the stairs.' His face twisted in pain and Zoe's gaze flicked instantly to the life pack.

'ST depression,' she snapped. 'Give him some more GTN and get a line in. He needs some morphine. Has he had aspirin?'

Teo stepped back as ambulance staff moved quickly to follow directions. He could see one of the students sitting on the back steps of an ambulance, crying. Someone was checking her ankle, which looked swollen. Turning his head, Teo could see a high ladder close to where the worst of the flames were. The shadowy figure of a fireman appeared in the closest window and something was shoved into the arms of the fireman still on the tiny platform at the top of the ladder. A bundle that looked like a baby.

Despite overseeing the management of the cardiac chest pain the old man was having, Zoe had seen it as well. She looked away from where the fireman was descending the ladder swiftly and caught Teo's gaze.

'You planning on hanging around for a bit?'

'You want me to?'

Her gaze clung to his for a heartbeat. She smiled. 'Please.'

She could manage perfectly well without him but she wanted him to stay. It was a little disturbing how good that made Teo feel but he didn't get much time to think about it. The fireman was on the ground now, running towards them. Zoe pointed to the open back of an ambulance and seconds later Teo was crowded in there, with Zoe and her partner and the firemen looking on as they tried to resuscitate a baby who was probably about the same age as Zoe's Emma.

The baby didn't appear to be burned but had inhaled enough smoke to go into respiratory and then cardiac arrest. Teo was given the task of finding a vein in the tiny hand as Tom and Zoe worked flat out, doing CPR and readying the defibrillator to try and shock a small heart back into action. The first attempt wasn't successful but they all knew this was just the beginning. No way would they give up on trying to save such a young life.

'We think we've got everybody accounted for,' a fireman said from the door. 'And the fire's almost under control. The baby's mother was downstairs, putting the rubbish out. She's pretty hysterical. There's a guy who says he's a psychologist looking after her. Want me to bring her over?'

'Not yet,' Zoe said. 'Maybe she could meet us at the hospital instead.'

'It'll be John Allen who's with her,' Teo said. 'He was walking to work with me and Luke. He'll take care of her.'

'If the scene's under control, I can step down. Find someone to drive us,' Zoe ordered the fireman. 'We'll transport under CPR. Teo—any luck finding a vein?'

'Still working on it.' Teo had the baby's hand bent over his fingers, stretching the skin on the back of it. He slid the needle in carefully and was rewarded with the flash of blood in the chamber that told him he was in the right place. He slid the cannula home. 'Got it.'

'Good. Stand clear. Shocking again.'

Zoe swapped places with Tom as extra crew members joined them. One climbed into the driver's seat to take the ambulance to the emergency department. Another was there to take over chest compressions. Zoe was preparing to intubate the baby now and Tom was drawing up drugs. It was crowded in there but Teo stayed where he was near the door. Zoe looked pale. Was it his imagination or did her hand shake just a little as she positioned the laryngoscope and the tube she needed to get into place?

Teo edged closer. 'How's it looking?' he asked quietly. It would be no easy task intubating a young child who might well have an airway swollen from heat damage and smoke.

'Can't see a thing,' Zoe said tersely. 'I'll have to go blind.'

The attempt was unsuccessful. Zoe looked up and Teo could see that this might very well be too much for her to handle. Of course it was. She was a mother and with the age of this child it had to feel like she was working on her own daughter. Unthinkably difficult.

'Let me try.' He didn't give her time to protest. He was, after all, the most qualified person here to be doing this and Zoe didn't need to know it was because he understood that she couldn't handle it emotionally—not that she was incompetent professionally. He'd be exactly the same if he had a baby of his own.

Just as well he didn't. And never would.

Zoe hesitated, though. Teo actually had to push her hand out of the way to take hold of the laryngoscope. He could feel how tense she was but this was a tense situation. He still managed to keep his voice perfectly calm.

'A guide wire would be good, if you've got one.'

She did. The tube slipped into place. By the time he'd checked the position of the tube and given the baby a couple of good squirts of oxygen with the bag mask, it was time to try defibrillating the infant again. They were also by this time pulling into the emergency department of the Harbour.

They got a rhythm. They took a few minutes before opening the doors to make sure the baby's condition was reasonably stable. It appeared to be, so as they unloaded the stretcher Teo stepped back. There were plenty of expert hands waiting to take over management inside the doors of the ED. He felt a hand grip his shoulder.

'You're a mess,' Luke said. 'Covered in soot. And have you seen what your clothes look like?'

Teo looked at his colleague and had to smile. 'Hey, you're not looking any better, mate.'

'Shall we find a shower and some scrubs?'

'Good idea. And then I want to check on how that little guy is doing.'

'I heard about him from one of the fire guys. Also heard that you and that cute paramedic made a good team. Going to follow up?'

'You mean on the kid? Already said that, didn't I?'

'No, you idiot.' Luke was grinning. 'I meant the cute paramedic. She's still in there now, isn't she?'

'Probably.' Teo wasn't going to let Luke know just how much he was tempted to muscle in on the team that would be at work in one of the resus rooms. To find a moment to let Zoe know that he understood how difficult the case must have been for her and tell her what a good job she had done. 'Might clean myself up first.'

He left it too late. By the time he went back into the emergency department, the only familiar face from that morning's incident he could see was that of John. He was with a white-faced young woman who had her arms wrapped tightly around her body, as if she were afraid something might break if she let go.

'This is Chloe,' John told Teo. 'Matthew's mum. Mattie's the baby who got rescued from the fire.'

Teo stilled as he heard Chloe suck in a very shaky breath.

'Teo's the doctor who was working with the paramedics to save Matthew,' he told Chloe.

One paramedic in particular, Teo thought. Only one came to mind, anyway... A hint of a smile tugged at his lips. And they'd saved Mattie? He was doing OK?

'Thank you,' Chloe whispered. 'I...don't

know what I would have done if...' Her voice trailed into a stifled sob.

'We're just going in to see how well he's doing.' John's raised eyebrow invited Teo to join them.

The doctor on duty was Mia McKenzie. Her long blonde hair was tied in a neat ponytail and she was listening to the baby's chest with a stethoscope. An anaesthetist was beside her, checking the settings on a ventilator.

Mia unhooked her stethoscope as she straightened and smiled at Chloe. 'I know this still looks scary but we're keeping Matthew asleep for a little while, until we know that he'd going to be able to manage his breathing on his own.'

Chloe nodded, her lips trembling. 'Is he...will he be...?'

'Babies are remarkably resilient,' Mia said. 'I'm confident he's on the road to recovery. He's going to go up to the intensive care unit now and they'll want to keep him there at least overnight so they can give him the best possible care.'

'Can I go with him?'

'Of course.' It was Teo who spoke. He turned to Mia. 'My team's on take today. I'll go up with him if he's ready?'

They both took another look at the readings on the monitors. Things were looking stable and Mia had every reason to sound as confident as she had.

'He's good to go.' She nodded. 'Thanks, Teo.'

'What's wrong?'

'What do you mean, what's wrong?' Zoe gave Tom a sideways glance. 'Isn't it enough that we're stuck in rush-hour traffic, going to what's probably a non-urgent medical job that'll we'll most likely have to transport when we're due to get off shift in exactly...' she checked her watch '...three minutes?'

'It's sure been a crazy day. Should have known

things would turn to custard after such a quiet start.'

It had been one job after another ever since the callout to that apartment block fire. Barely any down time for lunch or replenishing supplies. There shouldn't have been any time or energy available for anything else but Tom was right. Zoe had things on her mind.

Disturbing things.

Like when she'd seen Teo at that first job today. It had been so unexpected and it had caught her unawares; her body had reacted a split second before her head had. That tiny curl of sensation in her belly had come with a clear image of seeing Teo emerge from the surf the other day, sun gleaming on warm, brown skin. Wet board shorts clinging to impressively muscular thighs. That hint of a wild edge that his tattoo bestowed.

The shaft of desire was even stronger than the qualm she'd had on leaving Emma that morning. It was a sensation that demanded recognition in the same way that those other feelings had for days, now, when an echo of her baby's laughter captured her. Feelings that were like pinpricks of light coming through holes in a dark curtain. Zoe was accustomed to being in that dark place and the light was full of swirling dust motes.

Unwelcome? No.

Confusing? Definitely.

Part of her wished she could turn the clock back a year or more and that she could have met Teo when her life had been…normal. But she wouldn't have really met him, then, would she? He might have been present at that car accident but he hadn't stepped into her life until he'd rescued her in the waiting room that day. He'd rescued her again today, come to that. When she'd been faced with a task that had suddenly been overwhelming.

'I'm just a bit peeved, that's all,' she muttered aloud.

More like frustrated. Frightened, even. OK,

trying to intubate that baby that morning would have been a challenge and, yes, she'd had a bit of a wobble when she'd looked down at the little face and imagined that it was Emma instead of a stranger's child, but she would have got over it if she'd been given half a chance. She would have had to because the prospect of failing was terrifying. If she couldn't do her job properly, what did she have to hang onto that was still the person she remembered herself being? And now she couldn't know if she would have coped because Teo had stepped in and taken over. Shown her how it was done.

'What about?'

'I could have done that intubation this morning. Why do doctors think they can just take over like that?'

'Hey, the guy's a paediatric consultant, isn't he?'

'Yes.'

'So he was the best person for the job. What's the problem…you had something to prove?'

He *had* been the best person for the job and of course Zoe had wanted the best outcome for her patient but…how did he do it? Keeping a professional distance so easily? Did it come with the territory when you had to deal with small, sick children all the time? Kids were clearly a huge part of his life, both at work and at home. He wouldn't get a whole bunch of them following him around as if he was the Pied Piper or something, like he had at that barbecue, unless the love went both ways. And Emma had been the reason he'd stepped into her life in the waiting room. Not her. She needed to remember that, when her stupid reawakening hormones were making her feel things she wasn't ready to feel.

'Yeah…I guess.' Zoe pushed her thoughts away with a sigh. 'I still feel a bit rusty. And paeds cases are always that bit more intense.'

'Must be even more intense when you're a parent yourself.'

Maybe that was it. The reason why Teo could cope so well with children. This was just a wobble because it was the first paediatric case Zoe had had since she'd had her own child. Teo didn't have kids of his own and didn't seem to want any. Alisi had told her that.

'He won't even keep a girlfriend for more than a few weeks,' she'd confided sadly. 'I think my *ui* are going to be the closest thing to his own children that that cousin of mine will ever get.'

'*Ui*?'

'Piglets.' Alisi had dissolved into laughter at Zoe's expression. 'But in a nice way.'

'Here we are.' Tom's announcement was a welcome dead end for the intrusion of personal thoughts. 'Let's hope this isn't another paeds case for you.'

It wasn't. It was an eighty-seven-year-old woman called Agnes who'd had 'a bit of a turn' but had no intention of being taken to hospital.

'Your blood pressure's a bit low,' Zoe told her. 'And your heart rate's a bit too fast. You really need to get checked properly at the hospital.'

'I stay away from doctors, dear. Don't like them.'

'She went a horrible colour,' the neighbour who'd called the ambulance told them. 'All grey and pasty. I'm sure she would have fainted if I hadn't made her lie down.'

'I don't faint,' Agnes said firmly. 'Never have.'

'I think you came pretty close,' Zoe said. She was watching the screen of the life pack. 'You sure you don't have any pain anywhere?'

'I'm a bit short of puff, that's all.'

Zoe caught Tom's eye as he handed her the nasal cannulae so they could give Agnes some oxygen. It was probably only a mild heart attack that Agnes was suffering but there was no way they could leave her at home, and it could take some time to persuade her to come with them.

They were going to be late home tonight.

It was lucky that the Kangaroo Day Care centre was so accommodating. Zoe gave them a quick call when they were finally transporting Agnes to hospital.

'Emma's fine,' someone told her. 'There's no rush. We're open till 8 p.m., remember.'

Which gave Zoe an opportunity she'd been waiting for all day.

'I just want to pop up to the PICU,' she told Tom, when they'd handed the care of Agnes to the team in the emergency department. 'I want to check on what's happening to that baby we resuscitated this morning.'

'I'd like to know too.' Tom was more than happy to hang around a bit longer. 'We're off shift. I can grab a coffee in the staffroom.'

'Wouldn't have anything to do with that cute blonde nurse I saw you watching today, would it?'

Tom grinned. 'Go away, Zoe.'

'You'd better work fast. I won't be long.'

Teo was in the unit.

Zoe should have been prepared for that. Prepared for that swirl of conflicting emotions that were clearly going to happen every time she saw him. Only…she'd never seen him wearing scrubs before. The pale blue tunic top left most of his arms bare. The tattoo was hidden but Zoe knew it was there and knowing that made it feel oddly intimate. As if she had a small part of him that no one else around here did. The pleasure that came with the notion was another one of those disturbing feelings. Maybe she shouldn't have come here but it was too late to slip away. Teo had noticed her arrival as he looked away from the conversation he was having with another doctor near the central desk.

'Zoe…good grief, are you *still* on duty?'

'Just finished. I wanted to find out how our case from this morning is doing.'

'Good timing. We were reviewing him just now. Wendy, this is Zoe Harper. She was in charge of the resus on scene for Matthew.'

'I can't take the credit,' Zoe said, avoiding Teo's gaze. 'It was lucky Teo was there.'

Wendy's gaze travelled swiftly from Zoe to Teo and then back again. She smiled. 'Good team effort, then,' she said. 'He's doing well. We've got him sedated and ventilated to monitor his gas exchange closely overnight but we're pretty happy, aren't we, Teo?'

'Yes…I'd like to see a bit more movement on that end tidal CO_2, though. Do you think—?'

Zoe turned away as the doctors began discussing the technicalities of the respiratory support the baby was getting. She could see him, through the clear glass of one of the partitions. A tiny figure, lost on the expanse of crisp, white sheet. Naked, except for a nappy and a spaghetti junction of monitor wires and IV lines.

His mother was sitting beside the bed, holding one of the baby's hands. She didn't see Zoe staring because her gaze was fixed on her child and Zoe could understand why. If that had been Emma lying there, she'd be doing the same thing. Touching her child. Willing her to get through this and survive.

A sudden tightness in her chest moved up to constrict her throat and, to her horror, Zoe could feel the prickle of tears behind her eyes. She blinked and cleared her throat. That made Teo look at her again.

'Did you want to go and say hello to Matthew's mother? I'm sure Chloe would love to be able to thank you.'

Zoe shook her head. 'Not right now. I have to get going. It's way past time for me to be collecting Emma from day care. We had a late job.'

'I'll walk down with you. It's time I was heading home myself.'

Zoe found herself feeling more and more tense as they walked in silence to the elevators. She punched the button.

'Thanks for your help today,' she said, finally breaking what had become an awkward silence, her tone cool.

She could feel the surprised glance Teo sent in her direction. 'No worries,' he murmured. 'It was a tricky intubation.'

'I could have done it, you know.' Zoe stared

at the light above the elevator, waiting for it to glow. 'I was about to use a guide wire myself.'

'Would you rather I hadn't offered to help?'

The puzzled note in Teo's voice made her turn her head. Dark, dark brown eyes were watching her. Pulling her in.

'No, of course not.' Zoe swallowed. 'You were the most qualified person there. I just…didn't want you thinking that I was…incapable or something.'

'I would never think that.' The sincerity was palpable. 'In fact, I probably think you're capable of more than *you* think you're capable of.'

She was staring at him as the lift arrived with a 'ping' and the doors opened. They stepped in. The doors closed, shutting them into a small space. Alone. Together.

Zoe sucked in a breath. 'I don't understand.'

'You're a skilled paramedic,' Teo said calmly. 'That's not what I'm talking about.'

'So what did you mean?' Zoe knew her tone was sharp. 'That I'm not a capable mother?

Or…that because I'm a mother I'm less capable of doing my job or something? Is *that* why you took over this morning?'

Teo's breath came out in something like a sigh. 'OK, I did think you might be finding it tough dealing with a baby who was Emma's age. That it might be a bit close to home.'

'That baby was Kali's age, too. Did that bother *you*?'

'I'm used to it.' There was a curious shuttered appearance to Teo's face now. A barrier was up. It was an expression Zoe had seen before. On the beach, when he had dealt with the unpleasant task of causing pain to little Sefa by pulling off the damaged toenail.

And Zoe recognised that barrier. It was the way she felt about Emma. As though she was looking through a clear wall. Dealing with a baby that wasn't really hers. But she had no choice about that barrier being there. If she knew how to get rid of it, she would. Why would anybody want to keep it up?

Because that way they could do the kind of job that Teo did. They could have done Zoe's job this morning without the slightest wobble.

Was that what Teo meant by saying she was capable of more than she thought? Did he think she could take control of that barrier so that she could put it up at will?

Zoe wasn't sure she wanted to. That flash of feeling an empathy with both the baby and his mother had been...real. One of those pinpricks of light coming into the dark place. She couldn't pick and choose, could she? If she wanted to get mentally healthy and back to being who she wanted to be, she couldn't just choose to feel the good stuff. Like physical desire. Or baby laughter.

Dammit. It had been a long day and Teo was making her feel more confused than ever. Zoe didn't like it.

'You've got something against working mothers, haven't you?'

Teo shrugged. 'Doesn't seem ideal but maybe that's just because of the way I was brought up.'

'Emma loves day care.'

'And you're happy leaving her there?'

The elevator had stopped again. They got out and both walked in the same direction, towards the emergency department.

'I'm happy to be back at my job. Six months' maternity leave was enough.'

Teo shook his head. 'I don't think you've had maternity leave,' he said quietly. 'Maybe that's the problem.'

'What?' He thought she still had a problem? That made her feel...small in some way. Undesirable.

'You had sick leave,' he said carefully. 'Maybe maternity leave is exactly what you need now.'

Zoe's breath left her in an incredulous huff. Being told she still had a problem stung. She wanted to tell him to butt out. That it wasn't any of his business.

But she'd made it his business, hadn't she?

The moment she'd shoved Emma into his arms in the waiting room that day. When she'd agreed to go to his family gathering in case there was a secret of some kind that Samoans instinctively knew when it came to caring for and loving babies.

She couldn't say anything in the end so she just glared at Teo instead.

He simply smiled. 'Alisi was practically in tears at the airport yesterday, begging me to persuade you to come and visit.'

Zoe believed him. It had been the main topic of conversation on the shopping trip and she'd already had a text message from Alisi when she'd got home, to say that people were expecting her. Looking forward to meeting Teo's friend Zoe and her baby. Had it been at Teo's instigation?

'You're a lot better now,' Teo continued. 'If you had some real time with your baby, you might find the bond is a lot stronger than you think. That's what I meant.' His tone was gentle now. 'I think you're capable of being a fantastic mother but I think you're trying too hard at the moment. To be the best at everything. A few days in the sun with Alisi and you could really relax. You might even find that it's all a lot easier than you think.'

With a curl to his smile that made it almost a wink, Teo turned away, heading for the staff locker rooms. 'Think about it,' he called over his shoulder. 'There're some cheap flights going at the moment. I've just booked a few for myself.'

Zoe was left staring after him.

He made it sound so *easy*. As if there were no problems, only solutions.

And maybe he was right.

Things had changed for her since the barbecue. That was when the new feelings had begun to filter though into the numb place that was her soul.

Unbidden, an image of a tropical island came to mind. White sand beaches and palm trees.

The sound of singing and laughter. A glorious sunset with the silhouette of two people walking hand-in-hand on the beach.

Lovers.

She and Teo?

This yearning was a new feeling, too. Powerful. Disturbing.

Think about it? Dream about it, more likely.

And Zoe knew she was going to find it impossible not to.

CHAPTER SEVEN

IT WAS coincidence that both Teo and Zoe ended up on the island at the same time.

Or was it?

Zoe had known that he visited regularly to help out at the hospital. She had known that he'd taken advantage of those cheap flights and they were only available for narrow windows of time. She hadn't asked him if he'd be there when she'd impulsively booked tickets of her own the next day. How could she have, when she hadn't even seen him? She hadn't been at work and she'd been far too busy, anyway, organising a passport for Emma and getting packed. It seemed a huge effort to go to for just a few days away but Zoe had checked in with John to ask if he thought it was a good idea.

John had been enthusiastic. John was a friend of Teo's. Alisi was Teo's favourite cousin. There was no way he couldn't have known that Zoe was here in his homeland. If he'd wanted to avoid her, he could have done so very easily.

But here he was, walking towards where she was sitting under the shade of a palm tree on the beach. A good percentage of the village seemed to be accompanying him. Everybody aged under ten, anyway. He was wearing his board shorts and nothing else but that gorgeous smile of his.

Zoe's breath caught in her throat and her heart rate picked up with a thump. The fantasy of being on a tropical island with this man had been just that. A fantasy.

Until now.

'Hey… *Talofa*, Zoe. The kids told me I'd find you down here somewhere.'

The children were all staring at her with big brown eyes and wide, triumphant smiles.

Even a simple greeting failed Zoe. She could

only nod and smile back. She was basking in Teo's gaze. What did he see? One of her own new sarongs—a lovely dark green one with huge, white frangipani flowers on it. Bare, sandy feet. Skin that had taken on a hint of a tan but not without paying the price of far too many new freckles. Hair that was wildly curly thanks to sea salt and soft breezes. A hibiscus flower tucked behind her ear.

Teo was grinning broadly now. Leaning down towards her. His hand brushed her hair and Zoe could swear her heart actually stopped beating.

'Didn't anybody tell you which ear to put this in? The left side says you're married.' He pulled the stalk of the flower from her hair. 'The right side says you're single.' He threaded the stalk into the curls over her right ear. 'Available, even,' he added in a wicked murmur.

Zoe's mouth had gone very, very dry.

Was she available? For Teo?

Oh…yes…

Did he want her?

She had absolutely no idea. He was here, on the island, where he must have known he could find her, but there didn't seem to be any intimate message hidden in his gaze right now. He was relaxed and friendly and so…solid. So… Teo. A human rock. Just being close to him made Zoe feel safe. As if she could take on the world and succeed.

'It's great you could get here,' he said. 'Do you like it?'

'I love it.'

Simple words that didn't begin to say how much these few days had given her. A new way of life. A new family.

Paradise.

Maybe the words hadn't said that much but something in her face or tone must have told Teo much more. His smile softened.

'I knew you would.'

The children had got over that shyness that Zoe always seemed to instil for a minute or two. Now she was one of them again and their attention was on Teo. They were talking. Clamouring. Tugging at Teo's hands and legs.

'We're going for a swim,' he said. 'Want to join us?'

The thought of shedding her sarong to reveal her bikini made Zoe feel as shy as the children had been a moment ago. She ducked her head.

'I should get back to the village. Emma's probably awake again by now.'

'From what I saw, a fight will probably break out amongst the woman over who gets the privilege of looking after her this time.'

It was true. Zoe almost had to beg to get a turn with her daughter. Except for night-time, when they lay cuddled together on their soft mat to sleep.

'Alisi said you were staying in the *fale*. She did tell you that you were welcome to use my house, didn't she?' Teo was being swept away by a small sea of children. 'It has walls, you know.'

Zoe smiled. 'I'm right at home in the *fale*, thanks. I like being with everybody else.'

At home in the traditional, thatched roof dwelling that Alisi shared with her husband and children and extended family.

At home on this beautiful island.

At home. At peace.

'Come swimming with us,' Teo called.

She wanted to. She even got to her feet but something was holding her back. Had Teo expected her to stay alone in the house he had here, tucked amongst the tropical forest on a private beach? To be there, alone, when he came to visit?

Hope was the most delicious sensation. Exciting.

Dangerous because it could be trampled on and broken.

Zoe shook her head. 'I need to go and help with the *umu*,' she called back. 'They must have forgotten to tell me it's for your "welcome home" party.'

* * *

The village feast wasn't a 'welcome home' party for him. Preparations had begun well before Teo had arrived and no one had been expecting him today. Why would they, when one of his routine visits to help out at the hospital was only a week or two away? Not that they weren't used to him juggling tickets at the last minute when roster changes or something cropped up.

The impetus for this trip had sneaked up on him rather more slowly than the kind of things that usually prompted travel rearrangements. The excited text from Alisi the very day after he'd suggested that Zoe visit the islands had been more than satisfying. Zoe would love this place and a holiday, even if it was apparently only for a few days, would do both her and Emma the world of good.

It had been a couple of days later, when he'd known they'd arrived safely, that Teo had found himself becoming more and more distracted from his work. Thinking, way too often, about the Zoe he'd seen that day on the beach in

Coogee. Imagining her with the backdrop of his beloved homeland. Walking barefoot on a white, sandy beach. Watching one of the sunsets that had to be the greatest show on earth.

Alone.

If he hadn't given in to the impulse to check the 'grab-a-seat' website the next day, only to find a ridiculously cheap airfare available, he probably wouldn't have even considered the extravagance of popping over for a weekend.

He wouldn't be here now, with the smell of slow-roasting pig on its spit, watching Zoe learn how to wrap food in plaited coconut fronds and banana leaves before it went on the *umu*. The stone oven was good and ready now. He'd helped to prepare the glowing hot lava rocks before he'd gone down to the beach to find Zoe.

Now he was having a beer with the men of the village, trying not to make it obvious that his attention was firmly caught by how Zoe seemed to fit in so well with this part of his life. With his people. She stood out, of course, with her pale skin and flame-touched hair, just like Emma did where she was sitting in a group of babies being watched over by the grand-mothers. But even alone on the beach, in that *lavalava* that deepened the colour of her eyes to something he might find amongst the tropical greenery around them, Zoe had looked as if she belonged here.

He watched her helping the other women pre-pare the food. Then she went off arm in arm with Alisi and the two young women came back laughing, their arms laden with flowers they would use to make necklaces and crowns for this evening, and it was then that Teo realised he was seeing yet another side to this extraordinary woman.

Happy Zoe.

Absolutely, irresistibly gorgeous, *desirable* Zoe.

It became increasingly difficult not to set the old women's tongues wagging because Teo found himself drawn closer and closer to Zoe when the celebrations began. Finally, he gave in. With his plate laden with the wonderful roast pig and seafood, he went to sit beside her on a fallen log to eat, just outside the main group of people gathered around the bonfire.

Teo had been glancing at her plate often enough to notice how little she'd eaten.

'You don't like the food?'

'I do. It's delicious.'

'But you're not eating much.'

'I'm too…happy to feel hungry.' The statement sounded weird as soon as she uttered it but Teo merely tilted his head in acknowledgment.

'Contentment can be like that.'

What would he say if he knew that part of her contentment right now was due to the fact that *he* was here? Sitting beside her. Close enough for her to feel the warmth and strength of the hard muscles of his thigh through the thin cotton of her sarong.

'You're very lucky,' she told Teo. 'To have this

place to call home. To have family that seems unlimited.' She couldn't help sounding wistful.

Teo gave her a searching glance as he swallowed his food. 'What's the story with your family, Zoe? I know you said you didn't have any but I got the impression that you said that only because you didn't want to talk about it.'

Zoe could feel herself blushing. 'You see too much,' she murmured. 'It doesn't leave me anywhere to hide.'

'Why would you want to?'

She couldn't look away from him. Why? Because she didn't want to stop feeling this happy. This safe. What would happen if she told him the truth?

But he'd given her so much already. He deserved the truth. His gentle smile told her that she didn't have to hide. That he didn't want her to.

'My mother had several miscarriages before she had me,' Zoe said quietly. 'And then, when I was born, she...didn't want me.'

Teo sucked in a breath. 'Did she have postnatal depression?'

'It probably started with that but she went on to have full-blown psychotic episodes. She was in and out of a psychiatric hospital and on drugs for what seemed like my whole life. My father blamed me. My birth, anyway. My grandmother did most of the bringing up but she died when I was seventeen.'

'How is your mother now?'

'I don't know.' Zoe was ashamed to admit it. 'I left home when I was eighteen and I haven't had any contact with them since.'

'So they don't know about Emma?'

'I don't know. I wrote to them.'

'Are you going to call them?'

'I wasn't planning to.'

Teo turned his attention back to his meal, eating in silence for a minute or two, looking around at the crowd of people they were amongst. People who all seemed to be related in some way. Teo might not have his own parents any longer or any brothers or sisters but there were countless aunts and uncles and cousins and nephews and nieces. Real or honorary, it didn't matter.

'Family's family,' he said finally. Quietly.

And then he was silent again.

Zoe picked at her food, her appetite truly gone now. Teo thought less of her for abandoning her family but she still hadn't told him the worst of it.

'I'm scared,' she whispered.

He stopped eating. Zoe was staring down at her plate but she knew his attention was completely on her.

'What are you scared of?' he asked softly.

'Being...being the same as my mother.' There, it was out. The thing that terrified her the most about everything that had happened since she'd become pregnant. Longer, even. Maybe ever since she'd been old enough to know that her mother was different. Brittle and sad.

'Zoe?' Teo's voice broke into the darkening swirl of her thoughts. She looked up.

'You're not your mother,' he said softly. 'You're *you*. I understand now why you're so hard on yourself and I can see why it was almost inevitable that becoming a mother was going to be tough, but you're going to be fine. You're clever and talented and beautiful and Emma is going to grow up being very proud of who her mother is.'

His hand brushed her arm, tracing it with the backs of his fingers until he reached her hand lying beside her plate on her lap. It felt tiny and fragile as he curled his fingers around it and squeezed gently.

'You don't have to have the perfect house and an amazing job and pretend to be happy if you're not.' Teo's voice was just a whisper now. 'You just have to be you and Emma will love you, I promise.'

With another squeeze he let go of her hand. Zoe blinked tears from her eyes and sat very still for a long moment, trying to catch every word he'd spoken as it floated around her. They were precious, those words, and she wanted to keep every one of them.

She could hear the smile in Teo's voice now. 'How 'bout we go and get some of my Aunty Moana's banana pancakes? Don't tell anybody but they're what I really come home for, every time.'

She'd told him the worst about herself. Zoe would never forget James's horror at discovering she had a mad mother. Even if everything else had been perfect about their relationship, which it hadn't, that revelation would have been more than enough to have him running for the hills. But Teo had simply listened and accepted it and suggested they have dessert, as though… as though it didn't even matter.

It was bewildering. But wonderful.

Zoe let herself get drawn back into the group and found she was hungry after all. She finished her meal and then the sweet treats and then went with Alisi and the other mothers to settle the younger children in the *fale*. As she tucked a sleepy Emma under the handmade quilt, Zoe could hear the sound of drumming start up. By the time she went back, a group of young men was crouched close to the dying fire, intent on their music.

It was Alisi's husband, Rangi, who started the fire dancing. Traditional grass skirts were produced from somewhere for the men to put on and Teo was one of them. Holding sticks that were flaming at one end, he joined others to dance in front of the glowing embers of the fire to the intense tribal rhythms of the drums.

There were several men dancing but Zoe couldn't take her eyes off Teo. He'd stripped off his T-shirt and put the grass skirt over his shorts and the image was timeless. Primitive. Erotic. The grace of his movements. The thrill of the streaks of fire against the dark night sky. The sheer, raw masculinity of it all.

The party finished with the dancing.

Or maybe it hadn't.

Back in his T-shirt and shorts, Teo came to where Zoe and Alisi were sitting.

'Tired?'

Zoe shook her head. How could she be tired when she'd never felt this…*alive*? The drumming was still there. Coursing through her veins.

'Come for a walk? There's something I'd like you to see.' He held out his hand.

Alisi gave her a nudge. 'Go,' she urged in a whisper. 'I think he wants to show you the moon on the beach.'

'But—'

'I'll look after Emma.' Alisi's expression was curiously solemn. 'You should go with Teo.'

He led her along a forest track. It smelled warm and damp and there were occasional drifts of some deliciously scented flowers. There were scuttles of unidentified creatures and insects as well but Zoe wasn't bothered. Her hand was in

Teo's and she would have happily gone wher-
ever he was leading her.

It turned out to be a beach that she hadn't seen
before. A small curve of sand that was ghostly
white in the moonlight. The sea was so calm
there were virtually no waves, the moonlight
reflected in a path that led to the curl of soft
foam caressing the sand.

'My beach,' Teo said.

They discarded their sandals and walked the
length of it, hand in hand, letting the water wash
over their feet, deliciously cool. When they got
to the end of the tiny bay, they stopped and
looked out to sea, soaking in the sheer beauty
of it all and the warmth of the tropical night.
At least, that was what Zoe was doing. Finally,
she drew in a deep breath of utter happiness and
turned to thank Teo for showing it to her, only
to find that he wasn't looking at the moon and
the way it was reflected on the sea.

He was looking down at her.

His head dipped. Slowly. Slowly enough for

Zoe to know that he was going to kiss her. Slowly enough for her to have ducked her head and let him know that she didn't want that to happen and no offence would have been taken.

But Zoe did want it to happen. More than she had ever wanted anything in her entire life. The magnetic pull towards him was so strong she could feel her toes sink into the sand as her weight shifted, her body lifting to close the distance a fraction faster, her head tilting at the last moment so that his mouth could find hers more easily.

The first brush of his lips was so gentle. A soft touch that was barely there, and then he raised his head again to look at her. Zoe's lips were still parted. She had to run her tongue across them. To taste him. To make herself believe it had really happened.

He was watching her. His breath left his lungs in a low groan and Teo gathered her into his arms properly. And this time, when his lips touched hers, Zoe knew they weren't going to be taken away any time soon. They moved over hers, the pressure a dance all of its own, and when she felt the slide of his tongue Zoe could swear something inside her body started to melt.

It had to be her bones. That would explain why they both sank into a kneeling position on the sand, the kiss unbroken and gaining intensity so quickly Zoe wanted to cry out, but the sound was lost inside his mouth. Teo's hands found the knot on her sarong and it fluttered against her body as it fell. He stripped off his T-shirt and dropped it and Zoe saw the moonlight bathing his glorious, dark skin. She could still hear the echo of those tribal drums as he unclipped her bikini top and discarded it. She arched back as his hands covered her breasts, the sharp sensations in her nipples so intense they were painful.

She lay back as his lips salved the pain into pleasure like nothing she had ever felt before. She lifted her hips so that Teo could drag her last piece of clothing away and she reached for his shorts to help him. Her desire was a living thing now, the urgency overwhelming, but Teo stayed her hand and stifled her whimper with his mouth. He soothed and stroked her and made the pace more fitting to the slow rhythm of the waves beside them. Gentle and sure and...relentless.

Zoe had no choice but to be carried along, totally lost in the sensations. The exquisite pleasure. The sheer wonder that this was Teo making love to her on a private beach bathed in moonlight. When she cried out for the last time, Teo's cry joined hers. A sound of triumph and ultimate satisfaction. Two sounds that became one and were swallowed by the vastness of the tropical night.

Zoe had no idea how long they stayed like that, entwined on the sand. Still joined. Finally Teo eased himself away from her but they were still touching as he took her hand again. He led her into a milky-warm sea and they swam together.

The silence didn't worry Zoe at all. Talking aloud might have broken the magic of being here. She'd never swum naked before and the delight of it was like a dessert after the feast of Teo's lovemaking.

Even then, the pleasure hadn't ended. Teo dried them both with his T-shirt and spread Zoe's sarong so they could lie together on the sand again. This time they simply held each other and talked quietly. About nothing important, like what Zoe wanted to do on her last day tomorrow. About everything important, like what Zoe wanted for Emma as she grew up. And every so often, when they caught each other's gaze, they would kiss. Softly. With a tenderness that wasn't going to ignite renewed passion.

This was Zoe's last night on the island and she knew she would remember it for ever. Whatever happened back home, she wouldn't regret what they had just done. How could she, when it had been so perfect? Propping herself on one elbow, Zoe took a moment to simply look at Teo. To imprint the memory of this night in her head. She had to touch him then. She traced the marks of his tattoo with her fingers.

'Did it hurt?'

'Yes.'

'I understand why you have it.' Zoe leaned over to press her lips against the skin she was touching. 'It's a mark of who you are.'

'A chosen mark,' Teo agreed, his voice a soft rumble in his chest that Zoe rested her head against. 'It tells a story of the people I come from. My roots.'

His arms came around Zoe.

'Life leaves all sorts of marks on us,' he said. 'Frown lines, smile lines, stretch marks.' His hand left her back to touch her head. To stroke her hair. 'Sometimes the marks can't be seen because they're hidden inside but they're all important because they're the story of who *we* are.'

Zoe could feel tears slipping down her cheeks. He was talking about her history. The things that scared her. He was accepting her for what she was. Scars and all.

And in that moment, Zoe fell in love with Teo. So hard and so deeply that she knew there would never be any turning back. She *had* never, *would* never, love anybody as much as she loved him. She was his, heart and soul.

He just didn't know it yet.

CHAPTER EIGHT

ZOE looked...radiant.

That was the only word Teo could think of when he saw her again the next day. She was on the beach with Emma and she was holding her baby close and cuddling her and looking at her like all the mothers he knew looked at their babies. With *love*.

Whatever barrier Zoe thought she had that had stopped her bonding with Emma was obviously gone, and Teo's heart squeezed from the joy of it.

He couldn't take the credit. The bond had been there all along but Zoe hadn't been well enough to recognise it. He had helped, certainly, by showing her how to relax again and what family could be like. He had encouraged her to come here, to a place where it was hard not to find what was real. And maybe their lovemaking on the beach last night had also had something to do with it. Zoe had let go and allowed herself to feel.

She had been his for the taking.

Maybe she could even be his for the keeping?

His heart had been captured by this woman and her child even before the magic of last night. He'd stayed awake for a long time after he'd taken Zoe back to the *fale*. Pacing his house, alone and...lonely. But he'd done what he'd hoped to do that day he'd been so astonished at seeing the sad, frightened side of Zoe. She was on the right track now.

Happy.

This was when he needed to step back. To be her friend but nothing more because that's all he could ever be to any woman.

But it was so hard this time.

Zoe had seen him arrive.

'How do you do it?' she demanded. 'How do you make babies laugh?'

'Like this.' He scooped Emma from her arms and held her up, a chubby baby wearing nothing but her nappy. He blew a raspberry onto the soft, bare skin of her tummy.

Emma waved her fists in the air and shrieked with laughter. He handed her back to Zoe.

'You try it.'

Her eyes widened. She took Emma onto her lap. She bent her head and blew a very creditable raspberry onto her daughter's tummy. Emma's eyes widened even more than her mother's had. She didn't shriek this time but she giggled, a delicious gurgle that made Zoe laugh as well.

Teo's gaze was caught by the back of Zoe's neck. Pale, pale skin that hadn't been kissed by the sun yet. He wanted to kiss it himself. Then Zoe's head swung up and she was smiling at him. Right into his eyes. He could feel it, all the way into his bones. And he knew what that feeling was.

Love.

'Got your camera with you?'

'In my bag.'

'I'll get a shot of you and Emma.' He found the camera in the side pocket of the beach bag. 'Make her laugh again.'

'There might not be much room on the memory stick left cos I've taken so many photos.' But Zoe blew more raspberries and Teo captured the images.

'I'd like one of these,' he said. 'Man, I take some good photos.'

'I've taken some awesome ones myself. I can't wait to get them onto a computer and have a proper look.'

'That could be arranged. I'd like you to see my house before you go, anyway. That way you'll know what it's like if you ever want to come back and use it for a holiday.'

'Me too, Uncle Teo.' Alisi's little boy Sefa had come running from the surf. 'I want to see your house.'

'You've seen it before.' But Teo lifted Sefa into his arms for a bear hug. 'Of course you can come. Everybody can come. After lunch. Before we take Zoe to the airport.'

But the babies needed a nap after lunch and everybody else declared it was too hot to walk all the way to Teo's house so, in the end, it was just Zoe and Teo and Sefa who went. Sefa's little legs got tired before they got to the end of the forest track so Teo carried him piggyback until they got to the beach, where the little boy's energy suddenly returned and he had to run in and out of the waves at top speed as the adults walked on the damp curve of sand the receding tide had left.

Teo held Zoe's hand and, when he turned to share a smile at Sefa's glee, he knew they were both thinking about being here last night.

Being together.

The wave of longing caught him unawares. Desire he could deal with but this was much deeper. He wanted to be with this woman for ever. To see that smile every day. To feel her hand in his as they journeyed through life.

Maybe he was wrong to have cut himself off from that kind of love. That devotion that could be the heart and soul of one's life and give it the meaning and joy that nothing else could replace.

He opened his mouth, to say something to Zoe. To tell her he loved her?

He didn't know. And he didn't find out because Sefa chose that moment to come barrelling towards him and cling to his leg like a large, damp limpet. Teo had to pick him up again. He was still carrying the small child as he led Zoe into his house.

'Oh…Teo…' Zoe was standing in the living area of the house tucked into the edge of the forest. The wall's massive folding doors were open and the room and the wide deck beyond seemed to be a part of the beach. 'This is…gorgeous. Do you sit here to watch the sunsets?'

'Always.' The word came out with a curious gruff edge. Maybe it was seeing Zoe here, in the home of his heart, obviously loving it. Or maybe it was the feel of the child still in his arms. Teo could imagine it was one of their own children he was holding. Part of a family of his very own that lived in this house.

And it felt…perfect.

Blindingly perfect but, for just a few precious minutes, that didn't seem to matter.

It mattered a lot when Zoe was scrolling through the full-screen images of all the photographs she'd taken. Teo was fixing cold drinks for them all in his kitchen and he'd been listening to Zoe's excited exclamations.

'Oh…here's a gorgeous one of all the children swimming.'

'This sunset is incredible. I think I'll have it blown up to make a poster for my bedroom.'

'Here's Kali and Emma asleep together. They look so cute…like puppies in a basket.'

'Ooh…wait till you see this one of you with the fire dancing.'

And then Zoe went oddly silent. Teo added ice cubes to the lemonade and peeled the wrapper off an ice block for Sefa.

'Sit out on the deck,' he told the little boy. 'That way it won't matter when it drips.'

'Teo?' Something in Zoe's voice made Teo leave the glasses of lemonade where they were and walk towards her empty-handed.

'What's up?'

She was sitting in front of the computer and there was an odd stillness about her.

'Probably nothing but…'

'But what?' Teo was right behind her now. He put his hand on her shoulder as he leaned forward to look at the picture on the screen. He caught a whiff of Zoe's scent and lowered his head so that it was touching hers. They were both looking ahead at the photograph. It was a shot from last night, at the barbecue. One of the table, groaning with food, with the children crowded around filling their plates. Zoe clicked the mouse and there was another picture of the children. This time it was Sefa standing beside his big brother, Maru, beneath a tree. And then a closer shot of Sefa's wide grin and tousled mop of black curls.

Such a happy kid. Teo could feel himself smiling. He looked away from the screen to nuzzle Zoe's neck. Man…if Sefa wasn't sitting right outside, he'd just scoop Zoe up and carry her to his bedroom and make love to her. He'd—

'Do you see it?' Zoe whispered. The way she swallowed was audible. Or maybe Teo was only just becoming aware of the tension in her body. He blinked and looked again. And then his hand covered hers on the mouse and he clicked through all the images he could find that had Sefa in them. Back and forth until he got to that close-up of the little face.

How could he not have seen it? The flash from the camera was reflected in Sefa's eyes. One eye looked normal. The other eye had a distinct white circle in its centre.

It could mean nothing.

It could also be an obvious sign of a retinoblastoma, a rapidly developing cancer that affected the cells of the retina. And maybe it did have one of the best cure rates of any form of cancer but this was *Sefa*—a child who had a place in his heart like no other.

He'd been playing with this child only minutes ago. Giving him a treat. Having some stupid fantasy about him being part of a nuclear family of his own. And seconds ago, he was thinking of nothing but making love to Zoe.

Blinded by love.

For one mercifully brief but horrible moment Teo was taken back to when he was no more than a child himself. When his love had blinded him to what he had to do to protect the person he loved the most. His hand slipped from Zoe's shoulder as he straightened. He shouldn't even be touching her. He'd known the danger all along but he'd let himself ignore the warning bells.

There was no ignoring this.

'Sefa?' He walked slowly to where his beloved nephew was sitting on the edge of the deck, chubby legs dangling and swinging, his tongue out to catch the drips of his ice block. 'You nearly finished?' Teo ruffled the black curls on Sefa's head. 'We're going to take you for another visit. Would you like to go and see the hospital where I work?'

The flight back to Sydney was the first chance Zoe got to try and put the pieces of her day back together again.

The way it had started, with the glow of her love for Teo somehow spilling over or melting that barrier so that she was also, gloriously, in love with Emma as well seemed like a dream now.

With a sigh of pure relief Zoe realised those feelings were still there as they sped through the night sky into the small hours of a new day. She could see the back of Teo's head as he sat, two rows up and on the other side of the aisle. The last time she had walked past to go to the toilet Teo had had his arm around Alisi, who was sitting beside him, sobbing silently against his shoulder. Was Alisi asleep now? She had to be exhausted after the nightmare her day had turned into.

Just the sight of Teo's head…the memory of how it felt to bury her fingers in his hair as she helped bring their heads close enough for their lips to touch was enough to start that melting sensation in the pit of Zoe's stomach. And it wasn't just that she wanted to touch him again. To *be* touched by him. This was so deep there was no end to the love she felt for him.

He'd been amazing today. From that first, horrible moment of recognising the threat in that photograph, he'd been *so* strong. Sefa wouldn't have had any idea of the fear dogging their footsteps as they'd raced back to the village because Teo had kept him laughing. He'd sent him to play with his big brother while he'd talked to Alisi and Rangi and the senior members of the family. And then there'd been the car ride to the local hospital where a simple ophthalmoscope had been all the equipment a doctor had needed to confirm the possibility of a potentially deadly disease. Even then, Teo hadn't faltered.

'We'll take him back to Sydney tonight,' he told Alisi. 'We can't be sure until he has an examination under general anaesthetic and I don't want to do that here. He needs someone far more qualified than me to make a final diagnosis and start treatment.'

'*Treatment*?' Alisi had clearly been terrified. 'What kind of treatment?'

'I've been on the phone to Finn Kennedy, the director of surgery at my hospital. He's going to find the best ophthalmologist available in Sydney. In Australia, if necessary.'

Alisi was sobbing already. 'But what's going to happen?'

'If it is what I think it might be, there are several courses of action. Chemotherapy, radiotherapy, laser therapy or surgery. That's not for me to decide, though, Lisi. There are people who know exactly what they're doing. The cure rate is very, very high. Nine out of ten kids make it through this.'

'But I can't just send him to Sydney with you.'

'Of course not. You'll come as well. And Kali.'

'I'll help,' Zoe had put in then. 'I'll help you look after Kali and, if you're not at the hospital with Sefa, you can stay with me.'

Teo's nod and smile had been approving. Distant, perhaps, but Zoe could understand why he needed to pull the mantle of his profession around him like a cloak right now. He had dealt with Sefa's toenail like this, hadn't he? Putting the barrier up so that he could do what had to be done without having decisions and actions undermined because the patient happened to be someone very special.

He was being a tower of strength and Alisi certainly needed that.

And Zoe loved him for it.

When she tore her gaze away from Teo's head, it travelled only as far as the row of seats behind him. There were three children in that row, tucked up with the airline's pillows and blankets and all of them sound asleep. Sefa had been so excited at the prospect of an extra holiday with his Uncle Teo.

'Can we go to the beach again?' he begged. 'And play football?'

Such a dear little boy. Zoe stood up and leaned over the seats to check that the children were all fine. Very gently, she smoothed a corner of blanket away from where it was half covering Sefa's face. Her heart ached at the thought of what he might have ahead of him in the next few weeks.

Kali was flat on her back, her lips a cherub's bow and slightly parted as she snuffled in her sleep. Emma was curled up on her side, with one hand tucked under her cheek. The ache in Zoe's heart intensified and morphed into something new. Something so wonderful she could hardly believe she was experiencing it.

Mother love. The feeling that this tiny person

was the absolute centre of her universe. That she would—and could—do anything it would take to protect her.

There was so much love to be found in this small space of a few rows of seats. Teo and Emma, of course, but also Sefa and Alisi and Kali. These people were her family now and she loved them all.

She could draw strength from that love.

It was the new anchor in her life and Zoe knew she would need it in the days to come.

When was it that the way Teo could distance himself and be so utterly professional started ringing alarm bells for Zoe?

Maybe it had been there, right from the very beginning. When he had been standing behind her to look at the pictures on the computer. He'd been touching her. Nuzzling her, even, and then he had simply stepped away and he hadn't touched her since. Certainly not with his hands or his lips. Not even with a look that held any kind of special connection.

They'd arrived in the middle of the night and, of course, she would have expected Teo to take his cousin and the children back to his apartment. It wasn't as if there weren't any number of other places Alisi could use as a base given the amount of family they had in the city. At least Alisi was desperately keen for Zoe to stay involved.

'That would be wonderful,' she said, when Zoe offered to be with her when they took Sefa into the hospital later. 'If you're sure it won't interfere with your job?'

'I'm only casual. Doing holiday relief and sickness cover. I can just tell them I'm unavailable at the moment.'

Surely Teo would approve of her dismissing work in favour of being there for her adopted family? Or was it reminding him of her own dysfunctional family relationships? Out of kilter with her sleeping patterns now, Zoe found herself awake for a long time when she reached her own house. She even found herself with a pad of paper and a pen in her hand. Maybe Teo was right in the importance he placed on families. It was up to her to try and build a bridge and see if there was any chance of making a connection to her own roots again. She'd received a card in response to her letter to her parents telling them they were grandparents. Maybe she could take the next step and invite them to visit.

She wanted to tell Teo about the invitation she'd sent when she saw him the next day but it wasn't the time or place. Alisi needed her as an interpreter. It wasn't that her English wasn't perfectly fluent but Zoe could understand the medical jargon better and that way Alisi didn't feel stupid when she had to keep asking the same things over and over, to try and get her head around everything that was happening.

And Finn Kennedy was a scary person for someone like Alisi. Zoe would have been just as terrified, listening to the way he put things straight out there, without hesitation. Not that he was so forthright in front of Sefa but the little boy was already in the paediatric ward, being spoilt rotten by every nurse he smiled at.

At one point during those first couple of days Zoe went with Alisi for an appointment in Finn's office. The director of surgery had been behind his desk. Alisi and Zoe sat in chairs in front of it. Teo stood to one side.

'We've ruled out things like Coat's disease and toxocaracanis,' Finn announced. 'And the abnormalities are strongly suggestive of retino-blastoma. We're not sure yet if there's any optic nerve involvement so the next step is to do an MRI. I've also contacted a friend of mine in Brisbane, who's prepared to fly down for the surgery. He's a world-renowned expert in the field.'

'S-surgery?' Alisi stammered. 'What kind of surgery?'

'It may be possible to remove the tumour. It may be necessary to remove the eye.'

Alisi gasped and grabbed Zoe's hand.

'We'll know more after the MRI,' Teo put in. 'It may also be possible to start treatment with chemotherapy and if it shrinks the tumour there's another kind of procedure where it can be frozen. It's still possible that we can save not only the eye but the eyesight as well.'

He sounded as calm as Finn, Zoe thought. This was *Sefa* he was talking about. It just didn't seem right.

'We need you to sign consent forms for a lumbar puncture and a bone-marrow examination,' Finn continued.

Zoe's mouth went dry. So far, the worst Sefa had had to endure had been blood tests, an ultrasound and a general anaesthetic. She couldn't imagine how she'd feel if she had to sign forms giving permission to have a sample of Emma's bone marrow or spinal fluid taken. No wonder Alisi was crying quietly now. She squeezed her hand.

'They're needed to check for any spread of

cancer cells,' Teo told Alisi. 'We'll know more when the paediatric oncology team has reviewed the case later today.'

The case. It's *Sefa*, she wanted to shout at Teo but she couldn't because her throat had closed up in sympathy with Alisi. Tears were forming in her eyes and threatening to spill over at any moment.

'The odds are excellent.' Finn looked away from the distressed women. 'Isn't that right, Teo?'

'It is.' The affirmation was confident. Calm and steady.

So much so that Zoe looked up to see that Teo had stepped closer to Finn's side of the desk. The two men couldn't look any more different, Zoe thought. Finn was angular and rugged. He looked like he hadn't shaved for days and there was an intensity about him that was great if he was your doctor and was determined to cure you but there was no warmth of any kind of empathy there.

Teo was big and solid and…so much softer. She had seen this man play with children and cuddle babies. She had been made love to by him so she *knew* how gentle he was. How caring.

And yet, at this moment, the expression on his face was almost an exact match of the one on Finn Kennedy's face.

Determined.

And detached.

Chemotherapy for Sefa was started the next day. It was a major procedure because the cancer-fighting drugs were administered by a tiny tube that was put into a big artery and then threaded up into the optic vessels. Everybody hoped that the treatment would start getting results quickly but now that the initial rush of diagnosis and treatment decisions had been made, it was a matter of getting on with it and waiting.

It was hard on everybody and Zoe knew she was being selfish in letting it affect her so much but, with every passing day, she was feeling worse. She knew, without a shadow of a doubt, that however good a front Teo was capable of putting up, he was having to deal with something very difficult and personal. Maybe it was unreasonable to expect him to make time to spend alone with her but…she *loved* him. She desperately wanted to be allowed close enough to offer some comfort. Just to be there for him.

But he didn't seem to want or need her.

His department was only too keen to bend over backwards to help and he allowed that to happen. Sefa had a private room and there was a bed for Alisi in there as well. She was allowed to keep Kali with her most of the time and there was always someone available to help when she needed to be with Sefa for his treatment.

Word had got out amongst the Samoan community too and there was an endless stream of visitors and rules about the numbers allowed in a room at one time were often broken. These people brought gifts for Sefa and food for Alisi and they brought their love and laughter and prayers. While the friendship between Zoe and Alisi had deepened markedly over this period, Zoe's company was needed less often and that meant not even catching a glimpse of Teo when he was on the ward, tending to his small patients.

'You could go back to work,' Alisi told her. 'I'm fine, honestly. They seem to think that this treatment is working and I have Aunty Hina and everybody to help now. It's not that I don't love having you around but I'd hate it if we were making your life too difficult.'

It wasn't Alisi making her life too difficult. It was Teo.

What was happening between them felt like rejection and…it hurt. OK, life had happened and disrupted what had begun on the island but *something* had begun, hadn't it? Surely it wasn't just her imagination that had made her feel that it had been far more than some kind of one-night stand? If this was Teo's way of letting her down gently, it was unkind. It simply didn't fit with the man she was so sure he was, but if that was the case and she was going to have any chance of dealing with it and getting on with her life, she needed to know.

When she saw Teo out near the lifts as she left that day, Zoe took a huge breath, summoned her courage and walked straight up to him.

'We need to talk,' she said quietly.

There was a haunted look in Teo's eyes. 'I know,' he said. 'Look, I'm sorry. Things have been…'

'Difficult, I know.' Zoe wanted to reach out and touch Teo's arm but something held her back. 'But please don't shut me out, Teo. I want to help.'

He was shaking his head slowly. As if there was nothing she would be able to do to help him.

Zoe swallowed hard. Found some more courage. 'I don't understand,' she said softly, taking a swift look around to make sure no one was within earshot. 'I thought we were… On the island…'

Teo's gaze slid away. He actually shut his eyes for a heartbeat. 'That shouldn't have happened.' He opened his eyes again. 'I'm sorry, Zoe.'

'I'm not.' Zoe's heart was breaking but she could still feel the connection between them. Teo might not want it but it was *there*. Strong. Pulsing with life.

'Teo, I…I…'

I love you.

But the words caught. The connection might still be there but this wasn't the Teo she knew and loved, was it? There was a barrier between them that was as wide as an ocean. Unanswered questions about how and why he felt the need to treat Sefa as if he was just another patient. The child of a complete stranger.

'I just don't understand,' she whispered.

'Don't get me wrong.' A flash of something she recognised came into Teo's dark gaze and Zoe felt her heart lift. 'I think you're an amazing person, Zoe, and you're going to be a wonderful mother. You *are* already. Always have been, only you couldn't recognise it.' He sucked in a breath. 'You need a partner who can be everything you need him to be. Someone who can love you the way you deserve to be loved. I'm not that man. I can't be.'

The words came out before Zoe could salvage any pride. 'Why not?'

'It's not you. I can't love anybody like that.'

But he could. He did. He loved his family. And, just for a night, she had been so sure he loved *her*.

He must have seen the denial in her face. 'I won't *let* myself love anybody like that,' he said fiercely. 'It's a luxury I can't afford.'

Zoe had to take a step back from that vehemence. She shook her head in disbelief. Teo had shown her what love really was. She had opened her heart and, to her amazement, had become the mother she'd wanted to be, as well as this

man's lover. And now he was pushing her away?
What had she done that was so wrong?

Been estranged from her family? Well, she
was trying to fix that, wasn't she?

Was it because she'd been the one to spot the
sign that something was wrong with Sefa? No.
They all knew it was lucky to have been found
at this early stage.

Zoe tried to swallow the lump in her throat.
'We all need that kind of love,' she whispered.

'No.' Teo was rubbing his forehead so that
she couldn't see his eyes. 'It makes you blind.
You can't look after people.' He was actually
moving away from her now. Towards the ward.
Towards people he could look after?

Zoe fought the tears she knew would come.
She opened her mouth to say something but Teo
didn't give her the chance. He looked back at
her and his words were very quiet and utterly
final.

'I loved my mother like that,' he said. 'And
that's the reason she died.'

CHAPTER NINE

SOMEONE had once told Zoe that people get sent into your life for a particular reason.

Remembering that gave her something to think about while she waited for the kettle to boil to make tea for her unexpected visitors.

If it was true, then Teo had clearly been sent into *her* life so that she could fall in love with her own baby.

There were moments of such joy to be found now.

The soft, silky feel of Emma's skin when Zoe stroked a finger down a chubby little arm or leg. The miracle of those tiny fingers and toes and nails. The way her baby's gaze locked onto hers when she was being fed. Her *smile* and, even better, the gurgle of her laughter. Zoe was getting very good at blowing raspberries.

Those moments would always be here from now on. Zoe knew that now her love had been unlocked, it would never go away, it would only get stronger. Of course there would be times of frustration and sadness, anger and probably fear, but that love would be there as an undercurrent. Something she could tap into for strength whenever she needed it.

She had Teo Tuala to thank for that.

But the price she now had to pay was *so* high.

Yes, there was joy to be found in hearing Emma laugh but there was pain as well. Would she ever be able to hear that sound without seeing Teo on the beach that day? The way he had swooped her up into the air and bounced her, showing Zoe the real joy of being alive for the first time?

Her love for her daughter would always be there.

But so would her love for Teo.

And she simply didn't understand why he was pushing her away. What on earth had he meant by saying that his love for his mother had been the reason she'd died?

Zoe could remember the conversation she'd had with Alisi that day on the beach. Every moment she'd been with Teo and every conversation with, or about, him seemed to be etched into her memory with startling clarity. Alisi had told her that his mother had already been sick when she'd come to Australia but she hadn't realised it. That by the time they'd found the cancer it had been too late to treat it. He'd still been a child then. Did he think that it was somehow his fault that the disease hadn't been picked up early enough to provide a cure?

No. There was more to it than that. It had more to do with his other strange statement about love making you blind so you couldn't look after people. Somewhere there was the key to the way he could distance himself and be so completely professional when he was dealing with a member of his own family, like Sefa.

Zoe could understand why he felt he needed

to be distant to provide medical care but she still couldn't get a handle on *how*. She could have done it herself, in the early days with Emma, when her love had been in her head and not her heart, but now…there was no way she could distance herself. Just thinking about what Alisi had had to go through, being with Sefa while he had a lumbar puncture and bone-marrow aspiration, was enough to bring tears to her eyes. If it had been Emma, she'd have felt everything herself and it would have been infinitely worse, seeing it happen to her precious baby.

Finally experiencing the kind of love a parent could have for a child had changed Zoe for ever.

Being close to Teo, even for such a short period of time, had also changed her. His pride in where he came from and the way his family was such an important part of his life had been the catalyst for writing that letter to her parents.

And now, here she was, making a pot of tea to take back into her living room where her parents were sitting, taking turns holding their granddaughter.

Had they been sent back into her life for a particular reason?

No. Zoe had summoned them back, hadn't she, with that letter she'd written inviting them to come? And when her father had rung today to say that they were in a motel in Sydney, having come all this way to meet Emma, her first reaction had been one of horror.

What had she done?

The plea in her father's voice had been unmistakable, however, and a habit that had become ingrained ever since she'd come back from her brief holiday in Samoa kicked in. She could imagine that Teo was standing right beside her. Watching her. The desire to see approval warm that dark gaze was still a powerful influence, even now, when it appeared that the reason he'd come into her life was no longer valid. That the task had been accomplished and her life had to move on.

Did her future include her immediate family?

Taking the tray of tea, Zoe went back to the living room. Her mother was holding Emma and smiling brightly.

Too brightly?

Her father sat very close to her mother on the couch. He was leaning over Emma as he made faces, trying to make her smile. Emma obliged. She even reached up with a small fist and managed to knock his glasses off his nose.

John Harper laughed, sitting back as he pushed his glasses back into place.

'I think she might end up being a boxer.'

'No-o-o.' Celia Harper planted a kiss on Emma's head. 'She's far too darling to want to do something so violent. I think she might be a ballet dancer.'

'What do you think, Zoe?' John asked.

The stream of tea coming from the pot wobbled slightly. Zoe put it down. 'I just want her to be happy,' she said quietly.

The atmosphere became instantly strained.

Her father cleared his throat. 'Of course,' he said. After another heavy silence, he spoke again. A little tentatively. 'Are you happy, Zoe?'

She nodded. Talking about her postnatal depression to her parents was not an option because it would open a vast can of worms she was nowhere near ready to deal with. And she was happy. So far, she was even coping with the fear of a future that didn't include Teo. It hurt, of course, but it hadn't sent her plunging into depression and that, in itself, was giving her more strength.

'I have a beautiful daughter,' she said aloud. 'And a great job.'

She told her parents about her job as they drank the tea. She told them about her holiday in Samoa. When it came time for them to leave, she told them she was happy that they'd come to meet Emma.

'We're here tomorrow, too,' her mother said. 'We'd love to spend some more time getting to know her.'

'I'm working tomorrow,' Zoe said apologetically. 'Emma goes into day care.'

'Oh…does she have to? We could look after her.'

'No…' Zoe's headshake was definite. She found herself tightening her grip on her baby. 'I don't think so.'

Her mother bit her lip. Her eyes filled with tears but she managed to smile. 'I…understand, love. It's…all right.'

But it wasn't all right. Her parents went out to their rental car but her father came back to the door.

'This means so much to her,' he said. 'She's OK now. She hasn't been in hospital for years and she's even come off her medication, but her life has been…a bit empty, I guess. When your letter came, it was like the light came back on. She's so excited about Emma. So…*happy.*'

It was a shock to see that there were tears in her father's eyes. He loved her mother. They both wanted to love Emma. Was it possible there was still family to be found?

'I don't know when we'll be able to get back to Sydney. You did ask us to come and meet Emma. Is there really no way we could spend some time with her tomorrow?'

Zoe hesitated. She hadn't had the slightest doubt about leaving Emma to be cared for by Alisi or the aunties. And she *had* invited her parents to come and spend time with their granddaughter. What would Teo say if he could see her refusing to trust her own family?

'I'd be there every minute,' her father added quietly. 'I'd make sure she was safe, if that's what you're worried about.'

It was, but saying it aloud was too awful and might mean that she could never find a way of having her own family in her life. After an agonising silence Zoe found herself nodding slowly instead. Making the arrangements so that her parents could come and spend the whole day here with Emma.

Trusting them.

* * *

He knew she was in the department even before he saw her.

He had to glance up, of course, to see if that odd feeling of alertness was justified and there she was. Zoe was pushing one end of a stretcher into the emergency department, having been cleared by triage. Her patient seemed to have been assigned a bed close to where he was standing and Teo had to suck in a deep breath to steady himself.

It had been a couple of days since he'd told her he couldn't be the partner she deserved to have and it had been the hardest thing he'd ever done. It had been the right thing to do, he knew that, so why did it have to feel as though he'd ripped off one of his own limbs or something?

It hurt.

The whimper of the child on the bed beside him was like an echo of his own suffering but it also served to bring him back instantly into a professional space. He was standing beside

Evie Lockheart, who was doing an ultrasound examination on the abdomen of a small girl.

Ruby was one of the Harbour's well-known patients. The surviving conjoined twin had been an inpatient not very long ago, having extensive skin grafts to her hip area as a final repair after the separation from her twin, Amy. She had been doing very well but had been brought in this afternoon with a worrying history of severe pain and frequent vomiting.

She whimpered again now, even though Evie was being very gentle with the ultrasound probe.

'Hey, little one...' Teo tried to distract Ruby. Maybe he was distracting himself at the same time, because he could hear Zoe's voice in the background, reassuring her own patient as they prepared to transfer him to a bed. 'Did I hear your mummy say that you're going to school soon?'

Ruby sniffled loudly but nodded at the same time. 'I've got a pencil case,' she informed Teo tearfully.

'Awesome. What colour is it?'

'Pink.'

'Of course it is. That's your favourite colour, isn't it?'

'Mmm.'

'Teo?' Evie's voice was carefully neutral. 'Look at this.'

With another smile for Ruby, Teo turned his head to look at the shifting, shades-of-grey shapes on the screen as Evie angled the probe again.

'Definite obstruction,' he said quietly a moment later.

'Oh, no…' Ruby's mother groaned. 'Will she need surgery?'

Teo nodded. 'As soon as possible. We'll get her up to the ward very soon. She hasn't had anything to eat or drink in the last four hours, has she?'

'No…she's been vomiting since first thing this morning.' Ruby's mother looked close to tears. 'I can't understand why this has hap-

pened. I thought the grafts were the last procedure she'd need.'

'It could be scar tissue from the separation
that's causing the obstruction,' Teo told her.
'The surgeon will be able to tell you more later.'

'Who's going to be doing the surgery?'

'I'll get hold of Finn,' Evie said. She smiled
at Ruby's mother. 'I'm sure Mr Kennedy won't
want anybody else in charge of our Ruby.'

The young mother looked relieved. 'I wouldn't
want anybody else either. He might be grumpy
but he's the best, isn't he?'

'He certainly is.' Evie flicked a glance at Teo
that looked…oddly defensive? 'I'll call him
now, if you're happy?'

Teo gave a single nod. 'And I'll get a line in.
She's very dehydrated already.'

The nurse had to go into the adjoining area to
get the IV trolley and Teo saw Zoe look up and
smile at her. Then her gaze shifted a fraction
and she saw him and her smile faltered visibly
before she turned away.

Teo was aware of a constriction in his throat that made it hard to swallow. He'd hurt her, he knew that.

How could he have let things go as far as they had on the island? Getting that close. Making love to her had been a huge mistake.

But how could he not have let things go as far as they had? He'd been pulled closer at a relentless pace. It was astonishing how many images could be present in his head at the same time.

The fear in her eyes when he'd seen her in the paediatric outpatient waiting room.

The look on her face when she'd heard Emma laugh that day on the beach at Coogee.

Moonlight on her naked skin...

Teo had to look somewhere else. Fast. Evie was on the phone, presumably to Finn Kennedy, and something about her stance, or maybe the tilt of her head, made him remember that odd impression he'd had weeks ago that there was something going on between Evie and Finn that had nothing to do with their strained and frosty professional relationship.

Then again, maybe it had everything to do with it.

Maybe he and Evie had something in common. Perhaps they both wanted something they couldn't have because it would be wrong. Dangerous, even.

Evie hung up the phone but didn't move for a long moment. When she looked up, she saw that Teo was watching her and she held his gaze for a heartbeat.

Yes. There was something going on there and it wasn't something happy. Evie seemed to feel his empathy. Her smile was wry.

'He's going to meet us up on the ward. He's not very happy about being interrupted, mind you.'

'I guess he's tired too. We all had a hard night and it's been a long day already.'

'It's part of the job.' Evie straightened her

shoulders. 'You can't have a career like this without that kind of commitment.'

'Especially when you've had to work so hard to get it in the first place.'

'Yeah…'

The look acknowledged another kind of connection Teo had with Evie. OK, she hadn't had the kind of financial struggle he'd had to get through medical school and become a doctor but he'd heard that her father had been pretty obstructive. And he'd also heard that Evie had a very sick sister.

He'd lost his mother.

Maybe their reasons for letting a career like this become their lives weren't so different.

Maybe they could draw strength from each other.

Teo smiled at Evie. 'Let's get Ruby sorted and up to the ward.'

Teo was in the department.

Zoe had spotted him instantly, as though her

gaze had automatically been drawn in that direction. He had his back to where she was, apparently intent on watching an ultrasound that Evie was performing. Zoe turned her attention quickly back to her patient. She certainly wouldn't want Teo to catch her staring at him.

It wouldn't always be this hard, would it?

Could she get used to seeing him? Get to a point where it wouldn't fill her with longing and regret and this awful, dull ache that felt horribly like despair? It was bad luck that they were taking their patient into an area so close to where Teo was working but he hadn't noticed her. Either that, or he was ignoring her.

That hurt.

'Ready to lift?' Tom was on the other end of the stretcher. They seesawed the load higher until their patient would be able to slide across onto the bed. An emergency consultant came in with a registrar.

'This our SVT?'

'Yes.' Zoe nodded. She finished raising the

back of the bed so that the man could sit up, which would help him breathe more easily. 'This is Colin Jeffries. Thirty-nine years old. No cardiac history. He's got a narrow complex tachycardia with a rate of 200. Oxygen saturation down to 96 per cent.'

The consultant was smiling at her. Zoe smiled back. Luca di Angelo was new to the department but it was no wonder the gorgeous Italian doctor was turning heads in here. And judging by the sexual wattage in that smile, Zoe wasn't at all surprised by the rumours she'd heard of his womanising tendencies.

Luca had introduced himself to the patient and was talking to the registrar as a nurse hooked up the ECG leads.

'What do you think?'

'Valsalva manoeuvre?'

Tom caught Zoe's gaze. They had already tried that without success.

'If that doesn't work, we could sedate him and defibrillate. Or we could use adenosine.'

Tom nudged Zoe. 'Ever seen adenosine used?'

'Yeah…' The drug gave the chemical equivalent of the jolt of electricity a defibrillator delivered. 'Dramatic, isn't it?'

'I've never seen it,' Tom said wistfully. He checked his pager and then edged closer to the doctors. 'Mind if we hang around and watch?'

'Watch what?' The patient was looking alarmed. 'What are you going to do to me?'

'Nothing scary,' the registrar assured him. 'The first thing we're going to do is to get you to blow through this straw. As hard as you can for as long as you can.'

'Why?'

'Sometimes it's enough to fix whatever it is that's making your heart go too fast.'

A nurse came in, looking apologetic. 'Can I borrow the IV trolley for a minute? We haven't got one.'

Zoe smiled at her and stood back to let her pass. She looked up at the same time, only to find that Teo was no longer ignoring her. His face had that kind of detached, professional expression she had seen before. Like when he'd been with her and Alisi in Finn's office while they'd discussed Sefa's prognosis. The kind of look that said he was uninvolved enough on an emotional level to be able to deliver the medical care needed. The way he intended to stay uninvolved with anyone. Especially *her*.

Zoe tore her gaze away and turned back to watch the next stage of the management of Colin's SVT. She hoped her pager would go off. Tom would get another opportunity to watch the powerful effects of adenosine. Surely things wouldn't stay this quiet for much longer? She wanted to get back to the station in any case, in the hope of not being deployed on a late job.

Not that things didn't seem to be going well for her parents and Emma. She'd rung several times already today only to hear that Emma had had a nap and been taken for a walk to the park in her pram and that her parents had had no trouble in getting her to have her lunchtime bottle. Her father had sounded more relaxed with every call. Had he been expecting problems too? All Zoe wanted was for the day to be successful and…over. She wanted to get home and care for her baby herself. Maybe trying to have a career like this and be the kind of mother she knew she could be now was not going to work.

Colin had had two attempts with the straw to no effect. The ECG screen showed his heart rate to have increased if anything and he was even more short of breath now after blowing so hard into a tiny space. They were getting ready to use the adenosine, which was a procedure that needed careful management. The drug had to be injected into the right arm to get to the heart as fast as possible and it had to be flushed with a good dose of saline. It required two people because it took two hands to push the plunger on the large syringe of saline fast enough.

Zoe found herself as caught up as Tom as she

watched the medical team position themselves and then count down to administering the drug.

And, right at the critical moment, her pager sounded.

No…it was her mobile phone.

Horrified, Zoe slipped out of the resus area. She'd need to get outside to take the call because cellphones could disrupt things like IV pumps.

She couldn't help looking at the screen on her phone, however, and when she saw that it was her own home number, she had to answer it. Her father wouldn't be calling her mobile unless it was some kind of emergency.

'Dad? What's wrong?'

'Zoe…I…. Oh, God…I don't know how to tell you this…'

Zoe was near the glass board now. The place where Teo had introduced himself all those weeks ago. Where he had touched her for the first time when he'd taken her hand. The memory had no chance of making any kind of impact right now, however.

'Just tell me,' she breathed.

'Your mother's disappeared.' There was a catch in his voice that sounded almost like a sob. 'The car's gone too.'

Zoe could feel the blood draining from her face. She knew the answer to the question she was going to ask but she had to ask it anyway.

'Where's Emma?'

'Not here… I think…no, I know that Celia's taken her with her.'

'How do you know?'

'She rang. She said…she said…don't worry, I've got Zoe. I'm going to take good care of her.'

I've got *Zoe*?

Just how off the planet was her mother?

'Call the police,' Zoe said with icy calm. 'I'm on my way.'

Except she wasn't. Not yet. A curious buzzing sound was already filling her head so that her voice sounded like it was coming from a long way away. It was quite possible that she was going to faint, she realised. She held her hand out, groping for something solid to hang onto.

Something solid got hold of her first. Strong, solid arms. A face that was close to her own. A voice that sounded horrified.

'Zoe. What's wrong? What's happened?'

The buzzing in her head receded a little. Zoe used both her hands to push Teo away from her. Her breath came in short, sharp puffs as she backed away.

'Emma's gone,' she gasped. She stared at Teo, a maelstrom of emotion sweeping through her. She wanted to scream. She wanted to collapse on the floor and sob. She wanted none of this to have happened because she had no idea how she was going to be able to cope with it.

And she was angry, too. Angry with herself for having agreed to put her precious daughter at risk. Angry with her mother for being unstable. Angry with Teo because if it hadn't been for him, she'd never have invited her parents back into her life.

She was still staring at Teo. Her voice came out sounding nothing like it ever had before. It had all her anger and anguish and fear in her words.

'This is all *your* fault.'

CHAPTER TEN

WHAT was more shocking—the anguish in Zoe's voice or the thought that something terrible had happened to Emma?

At some level, Teo knew there was something else that was shocking. The knowledge that there was no way he could push Zoe and her baby far enough from his life to keep them safe. How could you push something away when it had become a part of who you were? The part that was responsible for keeping life going, in fact.

His heart.

He didn't question Zoe's accusation that it was his fault. Had something happened because he'd even considered letting himself love someone the way he loved Zoe? And Emma? Of course it had. He'd known the danger was there all along.

Except…it didn't make sense.

'What's happened?' He kept his voice low and calm, knowing that people all over the emergency department of Sydney Harbour Hospital were watching them both. Like Evie and her friend Mia. Luca di Angelo and Zoe's crew partner, Tom. Zoe wouldn't let him touch her, that much was obvious from the way she'd backed away from him, but he held her with his eye contact, willing her to let him closer. To let him touch her with his mind and heart, if not his body.

'I believed you…' Zoe's voice was a broken whisper. 'I thought, if I didn't have you, at least I could have my family again.'

'Your family? You mean your parents?'

'I believed you,' Zoe repeated. 'About how important family was. I let my parents visit. I gave them my trust and…'

'And *what*?' Teo took a step closer. The suspense was killing him. '*What's* happened, Zoe?'

'My mother's taken Emma. She's disappeared.'

'Oh, my God!' There was no stopping Teo from pulling Zoe into his arms now. He could feel the fear that was making her body rigid. She felt as brittle as a pane of glass that could shatter at any moment. 'What do the police say?'

'I…don't know. I don't even know if my father's called them yet.'

'That's the first step, then. Come on, I'll take you home.'

Zoe shook her head wildly. 'You can't… I…' She pulled away, looking around her.

Tom was nearby now, looking as horrified as everybody else. 'You go,' he told Zoe. 'I'll let Control know.'

Evie was there, too. 'You go too, Teo. I'll take Ruby up to the ward and hand over to Finn.

Go,' she repeated decisively, as she turned away. 'Zoe needs you.'

Did she? Teo still had his hands resting on her shoulders even though she'd pulled clear of his embrace. He could still feel that terrible tension in her body. She had nodded her thanks to Tom, with a jerk of her head, and was looking at him again.

There was desperation in that look. She needed him all right. But there was an edge of something even darker there as well. Hopelessness? Did she think he wasn't available for her?

There was no way he could even think of anything or anybody else right now. He was hers, a thousand per cent. His hands gripped her more tightly, drawing her closer.

'I'm here,' he said quietly. 'I'm here for you. We'll get through this together.'

His hand was her anchor.

Warm and strong, it cradled her hand as she sat beside Teo on her couch. She was close enough for the muscles of his thigh to be pressed against hers as well but it was his hand that was keeping her sane. The tiny movements of his thumb as it stroked her palm were a constant message of reassurance. He might not be saying very much but he was here. Totally here. As tense as she was about the whole situation but focused on protecting *her*.

They weren't alone in her living room. Her father sat on an armchair, his hand clutching his mobile phone and his head bowed as he stared at it, willing it to ring. Two police officers, a man and a woman, were also in the room. Daylight was fading now but Zoe couldn't bring herself to move and turn on any lights because that would mean letting go of Teo's hand and if she did that, she was afraid she would shatter into a million pieces.

The silence was unnerving. It made the house feel like an empty shell. Zoe could feel every inch of the space inside this cottage and how empty it felt because Emma was not there.

This silence had come after so many questions that had gone round and round.

'When did Celia disappear?'

'How did it happen?'

Her father had fallen asleep, that's how it had happened. On this couch.

'I didn't mean to,' John had said. 'It had been a long day what with the early start to get her so that Zoe could get to work on time. And we'd had that long walk in the park when we went to feed the ducks. I...I'm getting old, I guess.' He sounded old. Unutterable weary. Defeated, even.

'Celia said she was going to change Emma's nappy and I was sitting here waiting for her to come back and...and it just happened. I fell asleep. I'm sorry, Zoe. I can't tell you how sorry I am.'

'Why would she have taken off with Emma?' the police wanted to know.

'Because she's crazy,' Zoe had told them, not caring that she saw her father flinch.

'She's not crazy,' he'd defended his wife. 'She's had a long history of bipolar disease that has been difficult to control but…we thought we'd finally beaten it. She's been so good recently. You can talk to her psychiatrist…look, I have his number right here.'

Who would carry around a phone number for a psychiatrist if they weren't with someone they thought could tip over the edge at any moment? Seeing him take that card from his wallet had been a dark moment in this nightmare. Maybe John could sense that Zoe was thinking about it again now. He looked up and caught her gaze. Zoe saw him swallow hard and press the redial button on his phone. He held it to his ear but then looked away as he shook his head, killed the call and lowered the phone to his lap again.

Her mother's phone had been turned off. Hours ago now.

'Are there any friends or relatives she could have gone to?'

No. None. How sad was that?

'Where do you think she's gone?' The police had asked.

Home, was all John could come up with.

'She thinks that Emma is Zoe. She wants to take care of her. Where else would she go but home?'

It had taken far too long for the police to get to the key question. 'Do you really think that Emma is in danger?'

'*No*,' John said desperately.

'*Yes*,' Zoe said, with even more desperation.

People were out there, searching for the rental car. The police helicopter had been alerted and would be circling the vast city of Sydney until daylight had gone completely. Which would be all too soon.

The silence was getting heavier by the minute. This sitting around, waiting, was getting unbearable.

'I want to do something,' Zoe whispered. 'I can't just *sit* here.'

'There's no point in just driving around,' Teo

said quietly. 'Not until we have some idea of where they are.'

There would be a point, Zoe thought. She would feel as if she was trying. She would be away from this room. From the uniforms of the police and the broken-looking figure of her father that made her angry and sad. So angry. He'd promised he would keep Emma safe. He'd been with her mother for so many years, surely he could have recognised that some trigger had been set off? She was angry with herself, too. For trusting them. Her anger at Teo had faded, however. Yes, he'd made her believe in the importance of family but that was because he lived with the truth of it.

She wanted to be with *his* family right now. With Alisi and all the aunties. With that human raft of love and faith and unconditional acceptance that would surely keep any member afloat. At least she had Teo. She could only pray that that would be enough. Her love for her daughter was woven into her love for Teo and it felt like they were one unit. A family unit. She knew that Teo was finding this unbearable too. She knew that if heading out and taking on the world would bring Emma back safely, he would have been long gone. She could feel the waves of frustration coming from him in the way his hand tightened on hers occasionally. The way his face was set in such uncharacter-istically grim lines.

'She won't hurt her, Zoe.' John's low voice broke the new silence. 'I'm sure of that.'

'How can you be so sure? She's off her head, Dad. She thinks that Emma is *me*. That some-how the clock's gone backwards and she's got her own baby again.'

'That's why I'm so sure. She loves you, Zoe. She always has. She was terribly afraid that she might hurt you when you were a baby and she couldn't bear the thought of anything happening to you. That was why she had herself admitted to the hospital that first time. To keep you safe.'

'And what if she feels like that again? What

if she just abandons Emma somewhere to keep *her* safe?'

'An abandoned baby would be spotted quickly,' the female police officer said. 'People might not take a second glance at a grand-mother caring for a baby but they would no-tice something that's not right like a shot. We'd have calls coming in instantly if she left Emma somewhere.'

'I wish she would, then,' Zoe said, bitterness making her words harsh.

The crackle of one of the officer's radios made her jump and Teo's grip tightened convulsively until it was strong enough to be painful. The senior police officer unhooked the radio from his shoulder and spoke into it. They could all hear the message that was relayed to him.

'The vehicle's been located.'

'Where?'

'Parking lot at Strathfield train station.'

'Any sign of the occupants?'

'No. Engine's cold. It's been parked there for some time.'

'Anyone remember selling a ticket to an older woman with a baby?'

'Not yet. Trains are being checked. We'll keep you posted.'

'Roger.'

The police officers seemed more confident now. 'If she's on a train, there'll be plenty of people around her. She'll be on board for a couple of hours to get home. We'll find her.'

The female officer got up and turned on a light. 'Any chance of a coffee?' she asked Zoe. 'I can make it.'

'No, I'll do it.' At least it was something she could occupy herself with for a few minutes. She let go of Teo's hand and stood up. He shot to his feet as well.

'I'll help,' he said.

Teo closed the door of the kitchen as they went through it. He kept going towards where the electric kettle sat on the bench but then swung back, brushing past Zoe as he made for the door again.

He felt like a caged animal.

This was, potentially, a life-and-death situation and he was powerless to do anything about it.

Powerless to help the people he loved so much. Zoe.

And Emma.

He could feel Zoe staring at him, wide-eyed. Was he scaring her, unleashing this tiny fraction of his frustration?

'Sorry,' he growled. 'It's killing me, not being able to *do* something to help.'

'You are doing something,' Zoe said quietly. 'I'd be a total mess if you weren't here, Teo. Or I'd be attacking my father and blaming him for everything.' Zoe's face crumpled. 'And what good would that do? He already looks so...*broken*.'

'He's exhausted. Worried about his family. He

probably wants to be out there doing something too. Searching…*somewhere*.' Teo had reached the door again with his pacing. He raised his fist as though about to pound on the wood but controlled the movement with a supreme effort so that it made no sound when it finally made contact. 'Oh…God,' he ground out. 'I shouldn't be here.'

'*No*.' Zoe's voice sounded as agonised as his had. 'You shouldn't.'

He swung around to face her. 'Why did you say that? How do *you* know?'

'Know what?'

'That…that I've been here before.'

Zoe's face clouded with bewilderment. 'What are you talking about?'

'Sitting…waiting. Holding someone's hand instead of doing something. Not knowing what it is I should be doing.' Teo closed his eyes and rubbed at his forehead with his knuckles. His chest was heaving with the effort of sucking in air. He wanted to run. To hit something. To—

He felt Zoe's hand on his, pulling it down from his face.

'Is this about your mother?'

'No.' How could she think that he would try and make this nightmare about *him* instead of her and Emma? He shook his head to emphasise his denial.

'What happened to her, Teo?'

'She had cancer. She didn't get treatment.'

'Why not?'

'Because…because…she was ashamed of herself, I think. She'd gone against the family to come to Australia with her boyfriend and then he left her and we were alone. If she'd gone for treatment, they would have put her in hospital. They would have put me in foster-care.'

'But what happened?' Zoe was still hanging onto his hand and she gave it a tiny shake.

'She got very sick one night. I wanted to go and get help. Find a doctor or call an ambulance or something but she wouldn't let me. She wanted me to stay with her. She wanted to hold me. For me to hold her.' Teo dragged in a breath and the air seemed to burn his lungs. 'When she started having real trouble breathing, I tried to get away but…I was just a kid and my mum was a big lady.' Teo could feel his lips wobble as he tried to smile. 'You've seen my Aunty Hina? Well, Mum could have flattened her.' He tried to swallow past the lump in his throat. 'She only let go of me when she drew her last breath. And then I ran and yelled for help but…'

'But it was too late,' Zoe finished for him. 'Oh…*Teo*…'

'They told me it wouldn't have made any difference. That she would have died that night anyway, but how could I believe that? It wasn't true.'

'No…' Zoe had tears in her eyes. 'It wasn't true.'

Her agreement was so shocking Teo froze.

'It wasn't true because it would have made a difference,' Zoe said softly. 'Don't you see, Teo? Your mum died holding the person she loved the most. *Being* held. If you'd gone and called an ambulance, she might have died in an emergency department, surrounded by strangers. They wouldn't have let a little boy go in and cuddle his mum, would they?'

Teo couldn't say anything. He'd never thought of it like that. Never.

'And I told you that all this was your fault,' Zoe groaned. 'I'm so sorry, Teo. It's *not* your fault,' she added fiercely. 'And…you went for help for me. But this is completely different, don't you see? There's nothing you *can* do except wait and…and hold my hand.'

Teo was still stunned. Still hearing the echo of Zoe's words about his mother. And about something else.

'But you don't want me here,' he said slowly.

'That's not true.'

'You said I shouldn't be here.'

He could see the way Zoe struggled to collect herself as he reminded her of those agonised words. He felt her body stiffen as she let go of his hand and pulled away, nodding.

'For your sake, not mine.' She turned and reached for the kettle, tugging the lid off with one hand as she turned on the tap with the other. But she didn't fill the kettle. Instead, she put it down and turned back to face Teo.

'Look at what's happening here. How broken my father is. That's what happens when you love someone who has a mental illness. It breaks you. It breaks families. You don't...' Zoe drew in a shaky breath. 'I care about you too much to want that to happen to you. You were right. And it's a good thing that you don't let yourself love anybody like that.'

'No. I was wrong.' Teo reached behind Zoe and turned off the tap. Then he put his hands on her shoulders and held her gaze with his own. 'I thought I was right and I thought I was protecting you by thinking like that, but now I know how wrong I was. And I knew how wrong I was the moment I saw you looking like you did when you got that phone call in the emergency department today.'

'Like what?'

'So frightened. I know how strong and brave you are, Zoe, but right then you needed someone to stand beside you and do whatever it would take to protect you. And there's only one person who can do that.'

Just for a moment, it seemed that Zoe had forgotten what was happening around them here. He knew they would focus on Emma again within seconds but this moment was about *them* and only them. Zoe was listening to every word and the fear in her eyes had a glimmer of what looked like…hope?

'The person who loves you,' Teo continued softly. 'I was so wrong when I said I couldn't love anybody like that because I can. I already *do*. And…and you are *not* your mother. You're well now. You'll stay well but even if you don't, I'm not going anywhere.'

Of course he wasn't. Because how could he leave his heart behind?

'I'm here,' he added softly, 'because there's nowhere else I could be right now. *Ou te alofa ia te oe*. I love you. I love Emma. I'm not going anywhere. *Ever.*'

Yes, there was hope in Zoe's eyes but it was snuffed out in a heartbeat as the door to the kitchen opened behind them and the senior police officer stepped into the room.

'We've had reports in from all the northbound trains,' he told them. 'I'm sorry, Zoe, but there's no sign of your mother. We don't think she got on a train. Not to go home, anyway.'

'Where…? What…?' Zoe whispered. She felt Teo's arms tighten around her.

'So what are you doing about it?' Teo asked.

'We're widening the search. Checking other trains. We've got an APB out so all stations and patrol cars are aware of the situation. It's a matter of waiting. Hoping that Celia will get in touch.'

Teo could feel the frustration clawing at him again.

'Not good enough,' he growled. 'For God's sake, man. There's a baby out there who needs her mother. I'll get out there and start searching myself.'

'Let us do our job, son. You do yours.'

'What…sitting here and *waiting* while nothing happens?'

'No.' The police officer smiled gently. 'Looking after Zoe. That's your job and you're doing it well.' He raised an eyebrow as he backed out of the room again. 'That coffee would be great when you're ready.'

Teo was staring at the door as it closed again.

He'd just been given permission to do nothing but care for Zoe. To hold her and comfort her and…*love* her.

It was the right thing to do.

And maybe Zoe was right and it had been the right thing to do for his beloved mother as well?

The thoughts were confusing. They were

washing up against years of deeply buried guilt and sorrow. But they were wonderful, too, because it felt like absolutely the right thing to do to gather Zoe into his arms and hold her against his chest. To rock her gently.

'We'll get through this,' he murmured. 'Together.'

Zoe could feel the steady thump of Teo's heart against her cheek. She could feel the unwavering strength of the arms that held her. And she could hear the echo of his words, telling her that he loved her and he wasn't going anywhere.

Somewhere, amongst the new despair of the bad news of not finding her mother and Emma on a northbound train, there was something warm deep inside her.

Teo loved her. He didn't believe she was going to end up like her mother but even if the possibility was there, he wasn't going anywhere.

'I'd better make that coffee,' she murmured finally.

'I'll do the kettle,' Teo said. 'You find the mugs.'

It was when Teo snapped the lid back onto the kettle that he paused and looked at Zoe.

'Where would you go?' he asked suddenly.

'Home,' Zoe said.

'What if you didn't know where home was exactly? If you were confused?'

'What are you getting at?'

'I'm trying to think. Let's say your mother is confused and she really believes it's you she's looking after. That she's a young mother again with her new baby but it's all a bit weird. Where would you go?'

Zoe didn't have to use her imagination to conjure up the scenario. She'd been a new mother herself only recently and she'd been frightened and confused.

'I wanted my family,' she whispered. 'My mum.' She had to blink back tears. 'But I was too scared even to think about her. Too scared that I might see what I was becoming.'

'You weren't,' Teo said gently. 'You aren't. You're *you*, Zoe, not your mother.'

Zoe nodded. But she was thinking about something else. She was using her imagination now. Thinking of her mother nearly thirty years ago. With her own baby. Wanting her own mother?

She licked suddenly dry lips as she caught Teo's gaze again.

'I think I know where she might have gone.'

CHAPTER ELEVEN

'WHERE are we going?'

Teo was driving his car. They had made coffee for the police officers and her father and then said they needed to get out of the house for a bit. A change of scene. Some fresh air. They would have their mobile phones and would come back instantly if they needed to.

'Watsons Bay. I own a piece of land up there.' Zoe's hands were trembling in her lap. This was such a long shot and what if she was way off base? They'd be back to square one. Worse than square one because maybe this was the only possibility that offered some hope.

There was an astonished silence as Teo absorbed the information. 'You own two properties?'

'Only one house. There used to be a house on this land. It was my gran's.'

'Your dad's mother?'

'No. My mother's mother. That's why it only occurred to me after you asked me where I might go with a baby.'

'Why didn't you say anything to the police?'

'Because it might waste valuable time when they could be looking somewhere else. It's totally on the wrong side of the city from where she left the car. It would be quite a mission to get trains and buses from there with a baby but at least it's an idea. A place I *can* look.'

'*We* can look,' Teo corrected, taking his eyes off the road long enough to smile at Zoe. Then he frowned. 'Why didn't your dad say anything about it?'

'He's probably forgotten. It got left to me when Gran died and we weren't allowed to talk about it again. Mum said she didn't want it. She'd never set foot on the place again. It's not as if there's a house there any more. It's a few years since I went to look at it and there was nothing more than a burnt-out shell then. It's probably fallen down completely by now.'

'What happened to the house?'

'It was left empty for too long. It got vandalised. And then it was a target for an arsonist. I was at the point of trying very hard to leave my family and all the memories behind so I could start a new life. It felt…I don't know…cursed or something. I've barely thought about it again until tonight.'

Another silence as memories crowded back on Zoe. Her grandmother's protection had been wonderful but she hadn't understood her own daughter.

It's all in her head, for heaven's sake. If she had a bit of backbone, she'd get over it.

The acceptance of and treatment for mental illness of any kind was so different now. If her mother had had the kind of treatment and support Zoe had had, would that have made things better?

'Which way here?' Teo asked as they approached some traffic lights.

'Stay on Oxford Street. After Bondi, it'll lead onto the old South Head road. I could be wrong.' Zoe was twisting her hands together in her lap. 'It's only a possibility if it's really true that Mum's confused enough to think she's back in time. Before the fights.'

'What went wrong?'

'Gran was a wonderful woman but she was pretty old school and as tough as they came.' Zoe's smile was poignant. 'She told Mum she was being a drama queen and it was time she snapped out of it. That she didn't deserve a beautiful child if she couldn't pull herself together. She'd arrive and take me away to stay with her here in Sydney and then a few months later Dad would turn up and take me home again because Mum was out of hospital and couldn't stand the thought of her mother taking care of me. She stopped talking to Gran before I was old enough to really know what was going on.'

'And you got handed around like a parcel?' Teo sounded horrified.

'I loved Gran. She…*wanted* me. She loved me.'

'Your dad loves you. I'm sure your mum does, too.'

Zoe shook her head. 'Dad thought it was my fault that Mum went crazy in the first place.'

'What?' Teo took his eyes off the road again to flick an incredulous glance at Zoe. 'You are kidding, right?'

'No. I heard someone say it when I was about five or six. Some women from the church brought a casserole around when my mother had gone into hospital again. "It all started with her having that baby," one of them said. "That triggered the depression and it's been a downward slide ever since. No wonder John wishes it had never happened."'

'Malicious gossip,' Teo snorted. 'I've only just met your father but I can see how much he loves you. And Emma. He's desperate to look after his family. His whole family.'

'It didn't feel that way when I was growing up.'

'No.' Teo was silent for a minute. 'But we don't understand a lot of stuff when we're kids, do we?'

He sounded as though he had more on his mind than this mission. Of course he did.

Had he always carried the guilt that by loving his mother he had somehow contributed to her death? He'd become a man who had devoted his life to saving people. He even factored in a long journey back to the land of his birth at regular intervals to try and make sure what had happened to his mother never happened to anybody else. He wanted to be the one to pick up the early signs of something like cancer and ensure that one of his own people got the treatment they needed.

Good grief…did he feel the same way about Sefa? That he'd missed something he should have picked up? There must have been a point there when he'd been afraid of losing the little boy he clearly loved so much. No wonder he'd pulled his professional role around himself like a cloak. She could understand now and it felt like the volume of her love for this man had just been turned up to full power. Her heart ached for him. She would be there for him from now on. She would give him all the love he'd never allowed himself to accept since he'd been that lost, guilty child.

'Did you see Sefa today?' she asked suddenly.

'Of course.'

'How is he?'

'Doing really well. It's a fast-growing tumour so it's responding fast to the chemotherapy. Finn said he'd bring the specialist in to look at doing the cryotherapy possibly as early as next week.'

'So he's going to be all right?'

'Yeah…' Teo's voice was gruff. 'He probably won't even lose his eyesight. We have you to thank for that, Zoe. You're not going to believe the kind of party you'll be having the next time you're back in the islands.'

Would she? Would she ever party again if something had happened to Emma?

'Take the next turn,' she told Teo. 'There's a sign there for The Gap.'

Zoe felt her blood run cold as the words left her mouth. She gasped.

'*What*?' Teo swerved the car towards the curb and slammed on the brakes. 'What is it, Zoe?'

'I didn't think. I... Oh, my God...Gran's house is so close to The Gap.'

'What difference does that make?'

'Don't you know? You *must* know. You've lived in Sydney for so long.'

Comprehension was dawning. 'It's the spit of land that makes it look like a harbour entrance. Where that ship got wrecked way back.' His voice was trailing away. 'The place with the cliffs.'

Where about fifty people a year went to commit suicide. Zoe couldn't bring herself to say the words aloud. She didn't need to. With a wrench Teo put the car back into gear and put his foot down on the accelerator. The engine of the little sports car growled in response and responded with a smooth burst of speed.

Apart from the terse directions Zoe gave Teo, nothing else was said for the rest of the journey.

Because there was nothing else to say, was there?

The garden had been her grandmother's pride and joy but the masses of trees were overgrown now and made a suburban jungle that covered a large piece of land. What had once been lawns and flowerbeds was now a knee-high tangle of weeds. A kind of track had been trampled through the growth. Vandals? Her mother?

Zoe followed Teo towards the blackened stump of the old house. Surprisingly, it still had most of its exterior walls. Steps to the veranda were broken and dangerous and Teo kept a firm grip on her hand. With his other hand, he angled the torch he'd brought from the car. The small spotlight roved over what was in front of them. A desolate ruin of a family home. The front door of the house hung on one hinge and every window was a gaping hole with a few shards of broken glass.

'We shouldn't go inside,' Teo said heavily. 'It's too dangerous.'

Zoe was shaking all over now. Shivering with both the chill of the night and an unspeakable fear. If her mother had come here, she couldn't help but be forced back into the present time, could she? She would feel the emptiness of this house and know that it had been a very long time since it had been lived in. She would know that she wouldn't find her mother here. She would remember why.

She would feel…desperate?

Zoe felt desperate. Her mother wasn't here. Emma wasn't here.

She sank down onto the edge of the bottom step. She buried her face in her hands. Teo paced, shining his torch over the house. Around the menacing darkness of the garden. He wasn't going to give up. Not yet.

'There,' he said. 'Where would that go?'

Zoe raised her head. The cobbles of an old path showed between flattened clumps of grass. 'There're steps further down the hill. There used to be a goldfish pond and a summer house. And there was a gate that opened onto the track to the reserve. If you go far enough, you get to the cliffs.'

They were so far away from any other house that she could hear the way Teo pulled in a breath. The night was so still at this moment. So dark. So quiet and…dead.

And then they heard it.

A tiny whimper being carried who knew how far in the still night.

Zoe was on her feet in a heartbeat. Her heart recognised that sound. *Emma.*

Teo had heard it too. He was already moving down that old path.

Zoe caught up with him as he went through the gate. Hand in hand, they ran along the track. A public place this, and it was clear and easy to navigate. It led to a lookout. There were signs here warning people not to go past the fences but everybody knew how dangerous these cliffs were. Nobody went out of the safe area—unless driven by a force so powerful it was greater than the will to survive.

The way it had driven her mother.

Celia Harper was standing on the other side of the safety barrier. Only a few feet away from the edge of one of those famous cliffs.

Zoe was dragging in a breath ready to scream at her mother. She was gathering her strength to leap over the fence but something stopped her.

Teo.

'Don't rush her,' he said, his voice low. 'Stay right where you are.' He put his fingers across her mouth. 'Don't even say anything.'

Zoe pressed her own hand to her mouth as Teo's grip pushed her into a crouch. She wrapped her other hand around her body and stayed there, hunched and frozen. She had no idea what to do.

Did Teo?

He seemed to. He stood there silently for a long moment and then he spoke.

'Hey…you're Celia, aren't you?'

Her mother's head whipped sideways. 'Who are you?'

'I'm Teo.' He didn't elaborate any further. Was he trying to find out if Celia was back in touch with reality yet? Whether she knew that the baby she was holding was not Zoe?

Was he smiling at her mother? She was staring at him.

'Bit cold out here, isn't it?'

Celia nodded.

'Would you like to go somewhere warmer?'

She shook her head. 'I went to my mother's house but…' Another headshake, confused this time. 'But I don't think she's there.'

'I could help you find her, maybe.'

'No. She wouldn't want to see me anyway. She hates me.'

'Mothers never hate their children.'

'She thinks I'm weak. And she's right. I don't deserve to have a baby.'

Zoe's heart stopped as she saw her mother move but all she did was pull whatever was covering Emma into place.

'Nobody thinks you're weak, Celia. We understand.'

'No. Nobody understands.'

Maybe that was true, Zoe thought suddenly. Her mother had lived in a small community. She'd had her husband but the only other member of her family had been impatient with her and offered no compassion. Had her grandmother been afraid, as so many people were, that mental illness was somehow contagious?

How grim had life been for her?

Maybe her mother had never known what family could be like?

Zoe hadn't known, until Teo had opened that

door into another world. He'd made her baby laugh. He'd taught her to relax. She'd been so afraid. Trying so hard to cope and be perfect and the stress had made it impossible to include joy in her life. *She* had it now, thanks to Teo. Joy and the love that created it.

What joy had her mother ever had?

Had Teo caught something of her thoughts? He was looking at her now. There was a depth of compassion in that look. A touch of helplessness but also a strength that Zoe could hang onto.

She stood up very slowly.

'I understand,' she said. 'I've been there.'

Celia's head turned as slowly as Zoe had moved.

'Who…? What…? I don't understand…'

'It's all right.' Teo's voice was gentle. 'Everything's all right, Celia.'

'No…' Celia looked agitated now. She moved again and this time it was her feet. She stepped backwards and then turned. Towards the cliff.

Maybe Emma could sense the danger. Her cry was loud and demanding.

'Shh…' Celia rocked the baby. 'Shh, darling.'

Zoe started moving. She felt Teo's hand catch her arm but then let go.

'Mum?'

Celia stopped.

'It's horrible, isn't it?' Zoe said softly. She was edging sideways. Trying to get herself between Celia and the edge of the cliff. She could see Teo poised, ready to leap but undecided about whether it was the best thing to do. 'Feeling lost. Feeling like nobody understands.'

The baby's cries were getting louder. Celia swung her head from side to side. 'I don't know what to do,' she moaned.

'You're doing the right thing,' Zoe said. 'You're helping to look after Emma. That's what grandmothers do. But Emma needs her mum now. She needs *me*.'

'You…?'

'I'm her mum. She needs me. You're my mum. I need *you*.'

'No…nobody needs me.'

'You're family.' Teo's voice came from closer than Zoe expected. He was right beside her. 'We all need our family.'

Celia was staring at Zoe again. 'Who is this, Zoe?'

'It's Teo, Mum,' Zoe said. 'He's family too.'

She stepped forward and took Emma from her mother's arms. The sheer relief of holding her baby was enough to make her knees buckle but it didn't matter because there was a strong arm to support her. And Teo had a free arm. He used it to gather Celia close.

'That's right,' he said. 'I'm family and families look after each other.' He was moving them all away from the edge of the cliff. Towards a safe place.

A phone call would be all that it would take and they would have all the help they needed. The police. An ambulance that could take Celia to where she needed to be to get the kind of help that even Teo couldn't provide.

She could take Emma home and look after her and know that her precious baby was safe again.

That she herself was safe because she wasn't about to lose her daughter.

Or the man she loved so much.

Zoe snuggled closer to Teo's body. Help would certainly come and very soon, but she didn't need to be anywhere else to feel safe. Teo's arms did that for her and she knew they always would.

Overwhelming relief gave way to gratitude. Love.

Enough love for everybody. Even her mother.

'Teo's right, Mum,' she said softly. 'Everything's all right. Or it will be. You'll see.'

CHAPTER TWELVE

TEO had been so right about so many things.

About how she needed to relax and not stress so much.

About how she was not her mother and that she was in control of her own destiny.

About how she wouldn't believe the kind of party she'd be having the next time she was back in the islands.

A wedding party.

It was over now. The celebration and music and a feast. Emma was asleep, safely surrounded by what was now her own family. The couple at the centre of the celebrations had slipped away to have a quiet moment together.

Getting married on the same beach where she and Teo had first made love had been too perfect for words. In bare feet, with baby waves lapping at her toes and dampening the hem of the most beautiful white dress that had ever been created. Zoe still had the fragrance of frangipani coming from the flowers in her hair as they found themselves back on the beach. She had the warmth of a tropical night surrounding her and the colours of a glorious sunset painting the evening sky.

Best of all, she had the arms of the man she loved around her. His lips touching hers, his eyes holding the promise of everything she could ever want in her future.

'We'll have to do this again,' she said.

'What…this?' Teo kissed her again. Long and slow and so tenderly.

'Mmm.' Zoe smiled. 'Definitely. But I meant get married.'

'I don't think so.' Teo sounded very stern. 'I have no intention of getting *un*married, thanks very much.'

'Just another ceremony. Back in Sydney. So

that everybody from the Harbour can be there. So that…Mum can be there, when she's well enough.'

Teo nodded. 'Did I rush you? So much has happened in a very short space of time.'

'It's perfect.' Zoe reached up to touch his face. 'When something feels this right, why wait? It would be special to share it with people back home, that's all.'

'But this is home, too? Will you be happy spending as much time in the islands as I'd like to?'

'Being with you is my home, Teo. It has been, since I first met you. Being here in the islands is a huge bonus. I love it.'

'We'll have to come often for the next year or so. To supervise building that new wing on the hospital.'

Zoe's smile was joyous. 'Won't it be wonderful? Who would have thought that Gran's property would be worth so much? *Millions*.'

'You're a very wealthy woman, Zoe.' Teo's

smile was just as wide. 'Thank goodness you met me before you knew it.'

'Why?'

'Because with that kind of wealth I'd imagine you could get anything you want. Any*one* you want.'

'But I did.' Zoe stood on tiptoe to kiss Teo again. 'I want *you*, Teo Tuala. I was the richest woman on earth before I even knew about Gran's place. I will never stop wanting you. Loving you.'

A rogue wave swept in and washed around her ankles. Zoe squeaked and Teo scooped her into his arms. He didn't seem to mind that the trousers of his lovely dark suit were getting soaked. He stayed right where he was in the foam and looked down at the woman in his arms.

'For ever's not going to be long enough,' he said. 'For loving you.'

And then he kissed her. Again.

* * * * *

Mills & Boon® Large Print
Medical

September

FALLING FOR THE SHEIKH SHE SHOULDN'T	Fiona McArthur
DR CINDERELLA'S MIDNIGHT FLING	Kate Hardy
BROUGHT TOGETHER BY BABY	Margaret McDonagh
ONE MONTH TO BECOME A MUM	Louisa George
SYDNEY HARBOUR HOSPITAL: LUCA'S BAD GIRL	Amy Andrews
THE FIREBRAND WHO UNLOCKED HIS HEART	Anne Fraser

October

GEORGIE'S BIG GREEK WEDDING?	Emily Forbes
THE NURSE'S NOT-SO-SECRET SCANDAL	Wendy S. Marcus
DR RIGHT ALL ALONG	Joanna Neil
SUMMER WITH A FRENCH SURGEON	Margaret Barker
SYDNEY HARBOUR HOSPITAL: TOM'S REDEMPTION	Fiona Lowe
DOCTOR ON HER DOORSTEP	Annie Claydon

November

SYDNEY HARBOUR HOSPITAL: LEXI'S SECRET	Melanie Milburne
WEST WING TO MATERNITY WING!	Scarlet Wilson
DIAMOND RING FOR THE ICE QUEEN	Lucy Clark
NO.1 DAD IN TEXAS	Dianne Drake
THE DANGERS OF DATING YOUR BOSS	Sue MacKay
THE DOCTOR, HIS DAUGHTER AND ME	Leonie Knight

Mills & Boon® Large Print Medical

December

SYDNEY HARBOUR HOSPITAL: BELLA'S WISHLIST — Emily Forbes
DOCTOR'S MILE-HIGH FLING — Tina Beckett
HERS FOR ONE NIGHT ONLY? — Carol Marinelli
UNLOCKING THE SURGEON'S HEART — Jessica Matthews
MARRIAGE MIRACLE IN SWALLOWBROOK — Abigail Gordon
CELEBRITY IN BRAXTON FALLS — Judy Campbell

January

SYDNEY HARBOUR HOSPITAL: MARCO'S TEMPTATION — Fiona McArthur
WAKING UP WITH HIS RUNAWAY BRIDE — Louisa George
THE LEGENDARY PLAYBOY SURGEON — Alison Roberts
FALLING FOR HER IMPOSSIBLE BOSS — Alison Roberts
LETTING GO WITH DR RODRIGUEZ — Fiona Lowe
DR TALL, DARK...AND DANGEROUS? — Lynne Marshall

February

SYDNEY HARBOUR HOSPITAL: AVA'S RE-AWAKENING — Carol Marinelli
HOW TO MEND A BROKEN HEART — Amy Andrews
FALLING FOR DR FEARLESS — Lucy Clark
THE NURSE HE SHOULDN'T NOTICE — Susan Carlisle
EVERY BOY'S DREAM DAD — Sue MacKay
RETURN OF THE REBEL SURGEON — Connie Cox